Mercy's Birds

Linda Holeman lives in Winnipeg, Canada, and since starting writing in 1990 has written other children's novels, *Promise Song* and *Frankie on the Run*.

Linda Holeman

Mercy's Birds

Flyways

First published in 1998 by Tundra Books, Toronto, Canada
First British edition published in 2000 by Flyways
an imprint of Floris Books

British Library CIP Data available

ISBN 0-86315-317-8

Printed in Great Britain
by Cromwell Press, Trowbridge

Acknowledgments

With special gratitude to Melissa Kajpust, whose imagination and endless generosity helped this story come into the light. Thanks to my daughter Brenna for the title, and to Kathleen Allen and Lisa Dveris for so graciously sharing their information. And, of course, a large thank you to my friends at Tundra Kathy, Sue, Catherine, and Lynn, who took turns holding my hand through it all.

This book is for my son, Kitt, with love

These are the days when Birds come back —
A very few — a Bird or two —
To take a backward look.

Emily Dickinson

CHAPTER ONE

❦

"Get away! Go!" I banged on the glass. The pigeon started in alarm, flying straight up and then swooping down from the snowy ledge outside my bedroom window. I had been lying in bed, knowing that if I stayed there another two minutes, I would be late for school, but not really caring. Then I'd heard the soft, contented cooing outside my window. This was the third time I'd seen the pigeon resting there this week. I couldn't stand pigeons anymore. Not since last September, before we'd moved to this house.

Before that I'd loved them. Pigeons are everywhere in the city. Some people called them a nuisance, but I never did. For as long as I could remember, once spring came, I'd get a bag of stale bread and head out to the closest park. The parks I'd grown up in were just small squares of scrubby grass and weary old trees. There were always one or two green peeling benches, and maybe a rusting swing set, or a sandbox that roaming cats used as their own personal litter box. Peanut Park. That's what they're called, every one of those tiny, middle of the city parks.

Like I said, I had once loved pigeons. I would break up my bread and toss it on the ground around me, and then stand very still. Within moments, the birds would pass along their private message announcing food, and I'd be surrounded by their pecking, busy bodies.

"Mercy's birds," my mother and aunt started calling them. "Are you going out to feed your pet birds again?" they'd ask, seeing me leave with my paper bag.

I could never have a real pet; pets cost money to feed and look after. So those pigeons, who, like the Peanut Parks, all looked the same, were pretty much as close to having a pet as I'd ever got.

Then, that day last fall, I thought I'd try something different. I put a big chunk of bread on my shoulder, hoping one of the birds would land there. And one did. It grabbed the bread in its beak and sat motionless for a few seconds, maybe as surprised by its own boldness as I was. Then it tried to fly off, and that's when it happened.

My hair was long, halfway down my back, and still the colour I was born with blonde with the undertone of red that gives it the name strawberry blonde. The pigeon's sharp claws tangled in the hair on my shoulder, and the bird panicked. It flapped wildly, desperately, its wings hard and strong, beating against the side of my face so that I instinctively closed my eyes. I tried to stay calm, not move, but it seemed, even with the whirring noise of the wings, that I could hear the bird saying something harsh and urgent whispering into my ear.

And then it all came back, those times in the stealthy darkness, B's whispered threats and promises, and this time I couldn't stop myself: I opened my mouth and screamed, screamed the way I never could before. I don't know how long I stood there screaming, in the middle of that Peanut Park near our last house, the pigeon flopping around and tangling itself deeper and deeper into the side of my head so that we must have looked like someone on the cover of a tabloid: alien girl grows bird head, or human bird terrorizes children in Peanut Park.

I didn't open my eyes to see the person with the quiet, soothing voice, who cupped the pigeon's wings firmly, but gently, and unwrapped the tiny talons from my hair. I didn't thank the Good Samaritan, or say anything. I just kept screaming, even when I was free, and running. It seemed like my eyes were still closed as I ran, but they couldn't have been, or I wouldn't have been able to get home.

The next thing I remember was my own face in the bathroom mirror, one side of my hair all tangled and streaked with a ropy mess of green white pigeon droppings left by the terrified bird. I climbed into the bathtub with all my clothes on, knelt down, and held my head under the running tap, scrubbing and scrubbing, as if I would never get my hair clean again.

A few days later I was drinking a glass of juice by the kitchen counter when my mother walked in.

"Oh my God, Mercy, what did you do?"

"What does it look like?"

Pearl's cheeks sucked inward. "But why? Why did you do it?"

"I just felt like it, okay?"

"But your hair was always so ... you look totally different now, Mercy." My mother reached out to touch my hair, but I jerked away. "Older." She tilted her head to one side. "And harder. You look harder."

"I like it like this," I said, crossing my arms over my chest, and bending down to see my reflection in the kettle. In the dented aluminium, my face was that of a grotesque stranger, the features stretched and enlarged, the hair chopped off in rough bangs and reaching to just under the jaw. And it was black. Jet black.

I straightened up. "I'm keeping it like this, and there's nothing you can do about it," I said, uncrossing my arms and looking down at my hands. The cheap hair dye had left rims of black under my fingernails.

Nothing not bird claws, and not fingers, especially not B's fingers would ever tangle themselves in my hair again, scaring me, holding me prisoner.

CHAPTER TWO

Even though the sky had been clear on the morning I shooed the pigeon away from my window, a freak snowstorm blew up that afternoon the beginning of March, and everywhere snow was piling and shifting and blowing.

It was strange, moving around a warm, brightly lit glass room, surrounded by fragrant flowers glistening with moistness, while the outside world was dark and frigid and unwelcoming.

Anyone passing outside on the treacherous sidewalk, hunched against a wind that carelessly tossed handfuls of stinging pellets, could raise their eyes and see through the filmy layer of condensation me working in this small shining spot of colour and life. The florist shop was a magic tropical island in the midst of a winter storm.

They might envy me. They might think, *Look at that girl in there. Isn't she lucky?*

Earlier that afternoon, Mr Raymundo had informed me that it really was my lucky day.

"It's your lucky day, Marcie," he said, as I walked into my grade ten anatomy class.

"Mercy," I told him. "My name is Mercy."

Mr Raymundo blinked. "Oh, right. Mercy. Sorry. Well, Mercy, you don't get to find out all about the wonderful, mysterious workings of the digestive system. Instead, you get to visit Mrs Hardy-Spade. She's in Room 117." He handed me a small rectangle of pale green paper. "Guidance counsellor," he said. "But if you get back in time, you might not miss everything. I intend to make my way down to the small intestine by the end of the class."

I had been waiting for it to happen: the call to the guidance counsellor. The thing that surprised me was that it had taken so long in this school.

I went to Room 117 and knocked.

"Come," a voice said.

Mrs Hardy-Spade sat behind a desk, writing on a piece of lined paper. She glanced at me as I came in. The only word I could think of to describe her was "tidy." She didn't have a hair out of place. Everything matched. All her clothing, her hair, and her glasses were shades of brown.

"Molly?" she asked.

"Mercy."

"Sit," she said.

This was not going to be good. This very tidy woman had invited me in, checked if I was the right person, and told me to have a seat. All in three words.

I sat across from her and watched as she wrote, easing my key out of the pocket of my long sweater. The chair I was sitting in was one of those fake leather kind. Vinyl. With my hand tucked down under my thigh, I started pressing the point of the key into the vinyl.

Mrs Hardy-Spade put down her pen. "So, Mercy." Had she heard of prepositions? Adverbs and adjectives? She reached for the top file from a pile on her desk and opened it, her eyes crossing the page like a hungry lion tracking a herd of zebras.

I looked at her name again. *The Hardy-Spade will last you all season, I made up.*

It will not bend, even when digging into the toughest soil.

Something you'd see in a gardening catalogue.

"I'm sorry I didn't get to meet you before this," she said, tossing the file on to the desk.

So she could speak in complete sentences.

"I know it's been three months since you started here," she began, "but—"

"Over four," I interrupted.

She glanced back at the open file. "Right. But you didn't come to the Newcomers Group in December. Or the one last month. Why?"

"Why what?" I pressed harder with my key.

"Why didn't you show up?"

"I'm not into groups," I said. The key finally punctured the vinyl under my thigh with a tiny, satisfying plonk. I scraped my boots on the floor to disguise the sound.

Mrs Hardy-Spade sighed. "Look, this is a big school. Kids come; kids go. It's a transient neighbourhood. Our Newcomers Group is a way of meeting other students." She picked up the file again. "Have you made any friends?"

"Why?" I asked. "Do I have to?"

Mrs Hardy-Spade looked at the next page. "Your grades aren't too bad." Her right eyebrow raised.

"You elected to go into advanced English?" She looked across the desk at me as if she were seeing me for the first time.

"That's right," I said.

She looked down again, reading a bit more, then back up. "Any problems with teachers?"

I shook my head.

"Other students?"

I shook it again.

She took another sheet of paper from the file, and ran her finger along one line. "It helps," she said, still reading, "to socialize. Make a friend or two."

While she devoured the next line, I started on the next hole with my key.

"Under parent and/or guardian, you've named Pearl Donnelly." She looked up again, waiting for an answer.

"My mother," I said.

Her eyes flickered downward for less than a second. "And Maureen Grapko." Then up again, with that inquisitor's gaze. "Your mother's partner?"

"Her sister. My aunt."

"Anybody else in the home? Brothers or sisters? Other relatives?"

She was looking down again. I moved my hand up and slid the key back into my pocket. "Nobody else," I said .

B was gone, for now. All the way to Indonesia on a new site. He's an oil rigger. But he'd be back, he told us it was an eight month job. Then he'd be back, just before summer. Probably late May.

"I'll miss you, babe," he'd said to my aunt at the end of September, before we'd moved, wrapping his arms around her. Over her shoulder, he'd winked at me. "You, too," he mouthed. I'd turned my head away. All I could think of was that he was going. My aunt's boyfriend would be gone, and before he came back, I would somehow find a way to tell my mother, or my aunt, about the things he'd said to me. How he'd grab me by the hair when they weren't around, and pull me close to him, and whisper what he'd like to do to me. What he would do, soon. It was just a matter of timing, he said. "I'll be there, Mercy baby, when you least expect me." He also promised what would happen if I did try to tell.

Mrs Hardy-Spade shuffled more paper. A new page. I blinked, trying to erase B's face. I couldn't say his name, at least not in my mind.

I saw that the guidance counsellor was looking at me. Her eyes ran over my hair, my face, my black turtleneck. My hands, one resting in the other on my lap. A still, empty nest. "And how is everything at home?"

"Just fabulous," I answered.

She'd been at this for a while, this Mrs Hardy-Spade. She didn't smile, or relax back in her chair. She sat forward, her arms crossing and elbows leaning on the desk. Her shoulders hunched under the smooth brown fabric of her suit jacket. "Yeah, right," she said. Then, "Look, Mercy, I don't have time for anybody but the most needy students. In this place, needy students means kids who get into trouble. They don't show up at school, or if they do, they don't do any work. They disrupt classes; they get into fights. So far, that's not you." I saw that she had chewed off her lipstick. There was just a faint smudge of glossy pink in the creases fanning up from her top lip.

"So it's in your hands. You know I'm here, okay? I think you understand what I'm saying. I won't come looking for you unless I get a report from someone — a teacher, or an outside authority like a caseworker."

I nodded. "Is that it?"

"So you come back, if you have anything to ask about. Anything to tell me."

I stood up. "You bet," I answered, my voice slippery and smooth. I softly closed the door behind me.

I learned how the game works a long time ago. If you don't put the ball in their court, they have nothing to play with. I wasn't going to start telling any secrets to Mrs Hardy-Spade, this complete stranger. After all, I couldn't even tell them to my own family.

Talking about big things — things that were difficult to talk about was impossible at our house. It was easier to pretend they just didn't exist, and then maybe they'd go away. It shouldn't have been so hard to say what I was always thinking: *I'm afraid of B.* But it seems like my aunt is in love with the guy. And if it weren't for B, who knows where we'd be living? B has been helping out with money ever since he moved in with us, about this time last year, just before I turned fifteen. And he even left postdated cheques to cover our rent when he left. So. He makes my aunt happy because he treats her better than her two husbands and numerous boyfriends ever did; he makes my mother happy because her unemployment ran out around the same time B moved in, and his money was an excuse to stop looking for a job.

I did try to tell Pearl, the second time he came on to me. The first time I didn't let myself believe it really happened, thinking I was probably imagining it, or making something out of it that really wasn't there. After a day I told myself I'd made the whole thing up. But then he did it again, and I knew I was right about him.

"I don't like him," I whispered to Pearl, the second night he'd held on to me at the side of the house, not letting me go. Pearl and I were in bed. All I could see were the whites of her eyes, gleaming through the dark across the two feet of space between our beds.

"I don't really either," she told me. "But sometimes you've got to accept things you don't like. For other people's sakes. For Maureen's sake."

"But he's creepy," I said, sitting up.

Pearl sighed and turned over.

"Pearl," I said, to her back.

"Mmmm?"

"Don't you think he's creepy?"

Pearl didn't answer. I thought she'd gone to sleep. Then, "Lots of people are creepy, but he's paying our rent. That's all I know. So don't say anything to Maureen about him. As long as he stays, things are easier around here. Don't always think about yourself, Mercy. There are other people in this family besides you. I don't want to hear any more about him. Go to sleep."

I managed to stay away from him as much as I could, but there were times when I wasn't fast enough. Then he left, and I knew I had been granted this chance to really do something about the whole mess. I practised how I'd say it, over and over, before he got back.

Pearl (I never called her anything else), *Moo* (I always called her that), *I have to tell you something. It's B. He never leaves me alone when you're not looking. And he knows that I'm afraid of him, too afraid to tell what, up until now, have only been looks, and brushing against me, and whispering, and stroking my hair. But I know it's only a matter of time until ...*

It was just a question of finding the right words, and saying them at the right time. Timing, like B had said. It's all a matter of timing.

CHAPTER THREE

❦

On my way to work after school, ploughing through the blowing snow, I thought about Mrs Hardy-Spade having supper at home that night. She would be sitting at the table with Mr Hardy-Spade, or whatever his name was. He would be wearing a matching brown suit and brown glasses. There wouldn't be children, but a brown and white dog would wait patiently beside Mr Hardy-Spade's chair for any morsels of brown meat to drop from the man's fork to the floor.

"I had the oddest girl come in today," Mrs Hardy-Spade would tell her husband. "Spoke in two or three word sentences, and everything about her was one colour. Dyed hair, clothes, boots, everything black."

She would shake her head, and her hair would swing against the frame of her glasses. "No friends, no interest in meeting anyone. There'll be trouble from this one. It's all just a matter of time."

And Mr Hardy-Spade would reach down to pat the dog. "How do these kids get so screwed up?" he would ask, and then he and Mrs Hardy-Spade would shake their heads at each other across their perfect table.

Mrs Hardy-Spade was wrong about one thing. I did have a friend. She'd been waiting for me at my locker after school.

"*Another* earring? How many is that?"

I fingered the stud at the top of my ear. "This is the ninth. Four on each earlobe, and now this one."

Andrea leaned closer. "Your ear is sort of red and puffy. Does it hurt, way up there?"

"Not really."

"When did you do it?"

"Yesterday. After school."

"Doesn't your mom care? My mother said two pierces in each ear is the limit."

I shrugged. *Pearl? Care about holes in my ears?* "I might get one in my nose. A stud, here, though," I said, tapping the side of my nose. "Not that ring at the front." I hadn't really thought about it, but it just came to me, and I wanted to watch Andrea's eyes do that round thing that I like.

"Really?" All the white showed around the blue of her irises.

"Sure," I answered. Maybe I would, maybe I wouldn't. It was up to me.

"Can I go with you if you do? How do they do it? And what about sneezing and blowing your nose and all that?"

I shrugged again. "You can come if you want. If I get it pierced. But it's not for sure, yet."

"You're so lucky." Andrea sighed. She was always saying I was lucky, which got on my nerves, because I was not so lucky. But she really was okay. And she was my friend my only friend. Actually, my first real friend.

I thought back to the day I started at this school. October 31st. Can you imagine starting a new school on Hallowe'en? I don't know why I went that day; just that it was a Monday, and I didn't really give it much thought. We had been too busy over the weekend, moving all our junk from our old run down house to an even older and more run down house.

So I arrived at the school to find half of the student population in costume. I wandered around, finding the rooms whose numbers were typed on the sheet of paper I got from the office. It seemed to be such a strange and unnatural day that, for the most part, I just sat at the back of each class, looking at everyone.

The second day, as I walked into English lit, a girl's voice said, "Hey, in case you didn't know, Hallowe'en is over." There was some muffled laughter, and another girl's voice said in a stage whisper, "What's with her? Who is she?"

I slid in to my desk as if I hadn't heard, and opened the copy of *Brave New World* that the teacher had given me the day before. She said I'd have to hurry to catch up, as the rest of the class had already been assigned to finish chapter three. Pretending to ignore those girls, I also pretended to read as I sat up straight at my desk, even though I'd stayed up late and had finished the book after midnight.

During class I half listened to the teacher droning on about the first few chapters. I drew little pictures up and down the sides of the paper in my binder, and wrote lines and verses of poems I remembered.

When the class was over, this tiny wispy girl, her

heart-shaped face framed with feathery wheat coloured hair, came up to me as I was heading toward the door. Her eyes were huge, and deep blue.

"Don't mind her," she said, tossing her head in the direction of a group of girls laughing and pushing at one another as they went through the doorway. "Ignore what she said about Hallowe'en. That's Starr. She's like that to everyone new. Actually, to almost everyone. Just mean. I started here in September, and she bugged me for a while. I'm Andrea."

I put my hand up to brush my hair out of my eyes.

"Cool," she said, pointing to my black nail polish. "That looks good on you." She looked down at her own short, bitten fingernails. "It doesn't suit me," she said, then looked at my face again. "Did I tell you my name is Andrea?"

"Yes." I realized by her raised eyebrows that she was waiting. "Mine is Mercy."

"Marcie?"

"No. Mercy."

A wrinkle appeared between Andrea's eyebrows. "You're so lucky. I hate my name."

"Why?" We were walking down the corridor. Around us lockers banged and people yelled and a buzzer was going in the distance.

"I don't know. It's just ... ordinary. And people call me Andy sometimes. I don't mind if my family or friends do it, but when people who don't really know me that well think they can just ... you know ... take liberties with my name, I'm furious. What's your next class?"

"Geography," I said.

"Oh, you're lucky. I like geography, but I don't have it this term. Who do you have? Tobin or Schwartz? I hope you have Tobin; Schwartz just goes on and on. She's really boring; I have her for maths. Here we are; this is my class. But I'll probably see you later, around. Or maybe we have another class together." *Did she always have that intense look?*

"I guess," I said.

"And I love your boots. My legs are too short to wear high boots like that. You're so lucky." She flipped her head so that her hair swung out from her head for a moment, then settled back with almost a sigh, as if it gave up at trying to bounce. "Well," she said, "see you when I see you."

"Yeah," I said, and then went to find my geography class. *Sure.*

My mother used to say that to me when either she or I left the house. "See you when I see you," she'd holler. She wasn't big on keeping track of the time, so I took it to mean exactly what the words said. Not "see you after work," or "see you after school," or "see you in the morning," because our lives weren't as organized or normal as everyone else's seemed to be.

And Pearl was not what I would consider your normal mother, even before — before we moved to this last house, before she'd stopped talking to me, before she started fading away.

She had always been sharp tongued and somehow ... brittle, but at least she talked to me; talked and sometimes even laughed. She laughed the most when she was working on her crossword puzzles. She loved those things, and she had always made me help her when I was little. I remember looking up words in the dictionary and thesaurus, probably starting when I was back in grade two. I'd sit across the table from her, and she'd say things like, "Four letters. An ursine creature. Look up 'ursine' in the dictionary, Mercy. What does it mean? Hurry up. 'Bear?' Perfect! It fits." Or, "Six letters, third one *r*. It means 'lair,' *L A I R*. You know, where animals live. Look it up in the thesaurus." And I'd read out the list of words, and she'd shout, "Yes! 'Burrow.' That's it!"

Every time we got a word that she didn't have, she'd laugh and give me a high five, saying, "Way to go, partner," or "You're my own personal word-o-matic. Mercy, the word Meister." And I was so proud and happy to sit with her and help her, especially when she laughed. It was a hard raspy laugh, just like her voice.

Later, when I got older, I noticed that she'd stop herself in the middle of the laugh, as if she didn't deserve it. She'd stop, close her mouth, and put her head to one side as if she was listening, waiting for something. Pearl's life revolved around waiting. It could be for the next discovered word, for her next pay cheque, for the next spring, or even for her next cigarette. The most important wait was for the business she and Moo were going to open up.

She could bake any kind of pie or cookie or cake, and even more wonderful pastries with fancy foreign names like millefeuilles and baklava and palmiers. She didn't like cooking meals, but she loved baking.

She had baked for a living for years at a place called Highland Bakeries. So she was always planning her own place, where she could sell the things she baked either eat in or take out. Moo would have her own specially decorated room to do her job — fortune telling — with regular customers to keep her busy all day. Pearl used to tell me I could serve the customers, and she would pay me a third of the take each week. Way back then I believed her when she would tell me about her place and describe the colour of the walls and the style of the chairs and tables we'd have. Why shouldn't I? I had heard this story most of my life, and I guess back then, when she talked about it so much, I still believed in what she told me. And I'd see her experimenting at home; after each payday she'd go out and buy sweet butter and cream cheese and nuts like whole pecans and ground almonds and all kinds of delicious, expensive ingredients, and try out a new recipe.

For Pearl, it seemed that nothing was right at this moment. I knew, ever since I was little, that everything would be better when the wait, whether it was for the next cheque, or her own business, was over.

But then she had lost her job when Highland Bakeries went out of business, and all she could get was work at Robin's Donuts, which she hated because she couldn't bake anything there, just sell the doughnuts. Eventually she got fired. After a while she stopped looking for another job. She stopped doing crossword puzzles, stopped reading, or watching television. She just sat, and stared at nothing. She wouldn't even talk about the store she and Moo had planned, even when I brought it up. It was like that dream hadn't existed, or at least wasn't there anymore. And then one day I realized that even her face had a not quite there look, too. It was like that ice the kind that's deceptive, that looks okay, that fools you into thinking you can get across it. So you step on to it, and almost immediately you get that oh-oh feeling, and the next second wham! You fall into cold, wet nothingness, your arms flailing for the edge of something solid, your feet reaching down, trying to touch something firm and stable, but there's nothing there. Black ice, they call it.

CHAPTER FOUR

❦

By the time we locked up the florist shop, the storm was over. Now the snow wasn't falling, but was slowly being pushed into small drifts by the cold, persistent wind. Night had brought darkness, but the streets were bright in a strange way. All the lights from streetlamps, from car headlights, from house windows and the still lit stores were reflected, and yet dulled, by the new snow. The snow also muffled all the noise, and the world seemed oddly soft and quiet.

I stopped outside my house and looked at it before I went through the opening in the old fence that ran along the street in front. There were rusted hinges on one side of the opening, where a gate must have hung at one time.

Like the fence, the house looked like it hadn't been cared about for a long time. It was squat and old, crowded in between two other equally squat and old houses. When we had moved here, the landlord said he was planning to put on a new roof. Sometime.

"And what about the crack in the front window?" I had asked, pointing to it as he showed us around. "The window should be replaced. It will be drafty."

"Yes. You're absolutely right. I'll get around to that in the next few weeks."

The window was still cracked. Over it, the living room curtains were pulled shut, but they didn't quite meet at the middle. A sliver of pale light shone through, forming a long, light strip on the snow piled in the towel sized yard. The front door, warped in its frame and almost impossible to pull open, had a piece of cardboard taped on to it, telling everyone to PLEASE USE BACK DOOR.

Facing the house, you couldn't tell that there was a room at the top. The house looked like a one storey, but at the back it rose into a small gable with a window. It was really just an attic, but it was also my bedroom.

Apart from the finger of light, the house looked as quiet and still as the frozen world outside. The saying goes that it's the people inside that make a house a home.

I suddenly shivered and went through the opening in the fence, making my way around to the back door, trying not to slip on the icy sloping path that formed between our house and the neighbour's. The wind moaned through the narrow passage, pushing the snow ahead of it, and I knew that by tomorrow the path would be completely blown in, and I would need to break a new trail.

"What's that smell? Ugh. And it's smoky in here. Pearl!"

My mother was standing in front of the sink. Just standing there, staring at — what? Nothing. There was only blackness outside the dirty window. "Mercy? How come you're so late?" She still stared at the window.

I slammed the door behind me. "I told you this morning. I had to go to work right after school. I work until nine every Friday." I stamped my boots on the little strip of old carpet thrown down on the scarred linoleum at the back door, and hung my jacket on one of the hooks on the wall. "What is that stink? It's making my eyes burn."

"I wanted you to go to the store and pick up some toilet paper. We're out."

"I'm *so* sorry, Pearl," I said, emphasizing the "so," although my sarcasm usually didn't have much effect, "but some of us have to work. Remember work? Work equals money equals toilet paper. Get it?"

My mother turned away, her bony shoulders stooped beneath the old green sweatshirt. Her neck rose from the faded green like a thin white stalk. Since she'd cut her hair so short, her neck seemed longer.

I'm sorry, I thought. *Why did I say that? It's not your fault; it's not your fault. I take it back, Pearl.* I watched her bent shoulders, the way her feet slid, not lifting at all, as she left the kitchen and started down the hall. She moved as if she was exhausted. She always seemed tired, but I never actually saw her sleep. All she ever seemed to do now was lay on her bed, or watch the street from the living room window, ducking behind the curtain if anyone looked toward the house. She hadn't gone outside for a long time; it must be a couple of months now.

"I'll get some toilet paper tomorrow morning,

before I go to work," I called after her. "Where's Moo?"

My mother stopped, but didn't turn around. "Where do you think?" One hand gestured toward the living room, where pale blue light flickered out through the arched doorway.

I saw a round aluminium cake pan in the sink. Something black and shrunken was in the middle of the pan, as if it couldn't bear to meet the sides. Water had been run on top of the burned thing, and pooled in the dark hollows.

I looked around the filthy kitchen. "You said you'd clean this place up today." My voice came out hard again. "And didn't Moo buy any groceries? She said she'd get some stuff today. I left her money."

My mother moved down the hall again. "Get off my back, okay, Mercy?"

I was hungry. I was tired. I had a ton of homework to do. I felt sorry for my mother, but I was mad at her, too. "I'm so sick of all of this. This mess. Nobody doing anything around here. Buying food or anything." I was almost yelling.

My mother turned halfway around. "Don't blame me, Mercy. If you don't like the way things are, you do something about it." She turned away again.

"I will!" I yelled to her back as she went into her room. "Don't worry. I will," I yelled again.

I took a plain, hard doughnut from the cardboard box on the counter, and grabbed my backpack. As I went down the hall, I passed the living room and saw my aunt's unmoving bulk. She had fallen asleep in front of the television, her head on a flattened pillow on the back of the couch, her feet propped up on the coffee table. There was an empty glass tilting sideways in her hand. Her mouth was open, and because the volume on the television was turned off, I could hear little gasping snores. Then I passed my mother's bedroom, seeing her unmoving form, awake, on her rumpled bed.

Apart from the unmade bed, her room looked like no one lived in it. There were no pictures on the walls, nothing on the top of the old chest of drawers, or the dresser, or the little table beside her bed, except a lamp with a torn shade, and an old clock that hadn't been wound for months. The closet door was closed, and the heavy curtains were pulled shut.

I put the doughnut between my teeth, and pulled on the thick braided rope that dangled from the hall ceiling. With a quiet thud, a set of steep wooden stairs almost like a ladder pulled down, creating a square opening in the ceiling.

The house we lived in last year had been in better shape than this one, but it also had only two bedrooms. Before B came, I often left my bed, crowded in beside Pearl's, and slept on the couch, because Pearl had become so restless at night. She talked to herself, or in her dreams, and kept getting up and turning on the light, and digging through drawers as if she were looking for something lost. I could hardly ever get a full night's sleep, and then I'd sleep late in the morning and be late for school and get into trouble over that.

But after B came, and moved into Moo's bedroom with her, I stopped sleeping on the couch. Twice I woke up to find him in the living room. Once he was sitting on a chair across the room, watching me. The second time he was sitting on the end of the couch, his hand on the blanket covering my legs. After that I knew I'd stay in the bedroom with Pearl no matter how she kept me awake.

Then B had left at the end of September, and we were notified that the rent was going up November 1st, and even with the postdated cheques B had left, it wasn't enough. We had to move to some place with cheaper rent. I kept dreaming we'd find a three bedroom we could afford. We couldn't, but at least we got a house, and not an apartment like so many times before.

When the landlord showing us this place told us to step back, and yanked on the rope and pulled down the steps, he told us that while there wasn't a basement, there was "attic storage space." I'd climbed up and stuck my head through the opening. Immediately, I knew I'd found my own room.

I turned on the light and flopped down on my bed. I loved this little space, even though it was always pretty hot because hot air rises. The sloping walls were insulated with pink fibreglass with clear plastic stapled over it. When we first moved in, I had thought about taping posters and prints up on the plastic, but stopped myself, just like I hadn't let myself unpack all my cardboard boxes. A lot of it was just stuff from when I was a kid anyway nothing I really needed but I knew it would be a jinx to unpack everything, to get too comfortable, to make it feel too much like home. "We'll probably be gone by summer anyway," I had told myself. "It will be easier to move again if I don't take everything out."

So I had my mattress on the floor, covered with my favourite quilt. It was old and faded, washed so many times that it had grown almost silky. It was a patchwork quilt that Pearl said was called a crazy quilt. It had been hers, made for her by her grandmother, and when I was small and she'd tuck me in at night, she'd point out bits and pieces of material that had been her dresses and blouses and pyjamas when she was a little girl.

I also had a scratched wooden desk and chair, and I'd managed to get my long, low bookshelf up here, too. It was crammed with used paperbacks I had picked up at garage sales, and discarded hardbacks the libraries sold once a year. I didn't have a closet, but that didn't really matter. There was a whole row of nails on a board along the one straight wall, and when I'd moved in here, I'd taken down the strings of old Christmas lights and the garden hose and the ancient pair of men's skates that the previous owners had abandoned. The nails worked fine for clothes. Moo had given me a carpet that some old boyfriend the one before B had bought her; she didn't want it since it reminded her of him. It was soft and thick under my bare feet, swirls of muted greens and blues.

Sitting on my bed, I opened my backpack and took out a long paper cone. Unwrapping the crackly florist's paper, I looked at the flower. The white lily wasn't crushed, and the petals seemed unharmed by the cold.

I took it to my desk, to the big mayonnaise jar I used for a vase. The jar was full of flowers — roses and daisies and carnations and one of almost every cut flower we sold at the shop. I held the lily to my face. It was waxy and cool, and I breathed deeply, filling myself with the scent of somewhere else, somewhere far away.

Then I took the compass out of my backpack and went to the heavy plastic covering the fibreglass on my wall. I poked it hard, so that the point of the compass punctured the plastic, and then dragged it, slowly and firmly, downward, creating another long strip in the dusty plastic, matching all the other strips I'd made.

CHAPTER FIVE

❦

I put the toilet paper and bread and six oranges on the counter, glancing at the clock. Saturday mornings Vince opened at ten. I still had an hour before I started work.

Moo shuffled into the kitchen, tying the belt of her old pink terry-towelling robe. I noticed that there was barely enough material in the belt to knot it. The robe hung slightly open, and I could see that Moo had on her favourite nightshirt, the one with three penguins wearing red toques and scarves. Moo raised one shoulder and winced. "I fell asleep on the couch, and slept there until four this morning. I feel like someone's been wringing my neck." She reached up and massaged the side of her neck.

"I know. I saw you."

"Why didn't you wake me up so I could go to bed?"

"Wake you up to tell you to go to sleep? That's a bit ridiculous."

"You know what I mean. Hey, Mercy, let me read your cards." She kept rubbing at her neck. "I feel awful. Is there any coffee?"

She did look awful. "I didn't make any." I took one of the oranges and started peeling it. "And why would you want to do a reading first thing in the morning?"

"I had this dream. It was very prophetic. I can feel all my senses surging. That's a sure sign that something big is about to happen. Come on."

"I don't feel like it. I have to go to work soon. Do Pearl's."

Moo looked over her shoulder, toward the hall and Pearl's closed door. "No. She probably won't come out for hours. And anyway, she said she doesn't want me talking about her future anymore, or reading anything for her."

My aunt reads. She's the one who got me my first library card. She used to read books all the time, and tell me about them, although lately she just seems to watch television. But she reads other things, too palms, teacups, and tarot cards. She even makes a meagre living at it, and calls herself a reader of the future. An oracle, a seer. It sounds so much better than part time waitress slash occasional fortune teller.

"The last time she let me do a reading," Moo went on, "was a few weeks ago. She doesn't seem to care anymore."

"What else is new?" I asked, not expecting an answer. I separated the orange into wedges and arranged them on a plate so that the ends were all together in the middle. They made an orange flower.

"Mercy? Can you go and try to get her up? Maybe she'll listen to you and stop being in such a bad mood." I looked down at my flower orange. *Bad mood? Moo called it a bad mood?* "It's not right, Mercy. She lays there all day. For the last few weeks I've hardly been able to get her to take a shower, or change her clothes." Moo fingered the knot of her belt. "I've never seen her have the blues for so long."

"Has she been eating anything more?"

Moo shook her head, then grimaced and grabbed her neck again, groaning. "I don't know which feels worse. My neck or my head."

"I bought some oranges," I said. "I shouldn't have, because they're expensive right now. But I know she likes oranges. Try to make her eat one today."

Moo ran water into the coffeepot. She spooned coffee grains into the little metal basket and fit it into the top of the pot, then put the pot on the stove. All her movements were slow. Her hands were shaky.

I watched her, seeing how the bathrobe strained across her thick back. She seemed bigger than ever. She was getting bigger, and my mother was getting smaller. If you merged them together, and then separated them evenly down the centre, you'd have two normal sized people. But my aunt was like a balloon, gradually stretching and filling, rounder and firmer.

And Pearl, my mother, was like sugar in water, scattering and getting thinner and more transparent until eventually, she might totally dissolve.

"Please? Pretty please, Mercy, let me do your cards? It will make me forget about this headache."

The coffee was burbling on the stove. I took the last segment of the orange and put it in my mouth, biting it slowly to let its juice burst over my tongue as the last ten pieces had. The taste reminded me of summer. I looked at my aunt in her threadbare bathrobe, her feet bare on the cold kitchen linoleum. Her toenails were painted fuchsia. Her lips looked puffy this morning; she reminded me of a very large, sulky child, who was too big for her clothes.

"Oh, alright," I said, swallowing the last bit of the orange. "But a really quick one. That's all I have time for."

Moo flashed me the thumbs up sign, beaming. "My cards are on my dresser. We'll do the five card spread."

I went into her room, stepping through the maze of clothes on the floor. I picked up the deck of cards wrapped in a rectangle of white silk. The top of her dresser was crammed with bottles and jars and tubes some empty, some with the tops off. There were all kinds of things for Moo's skin and hair cleansing creams and masques and moisturizers and hairspray and mousse. There was make-up: a rainbow of eyeshadow and concealers and foundation and blush and mascara and too many lipsticks to count. There were also bottles of perfume. In the midst of it all were a few framed pictures. One of them was my grandmother, Moo and Pearl's mother. I had never met her, or even seen a recent picture of her. This picture was old, black and white, obviously taken long before the young woman became my grandmother, or probably even a mother. She was sitting on a lawn chair, grinning, her front top teeth crooked and crowding over one another. A bird sat on top of her head something small a budgie, I think.

In another of the frames on Moo's dresser was a

picture of the three of us, Moo and Pearl and me, sitting on the front steps of our last house. B had taken it last summer. Moo's whole face was one big smile. Pearl and I were just looking at the camera.

In the mirror over the dresser I tried to copy Moo's smile. But it looked like I was baring my teeth, ready to chomp into someone's jugular. Then I smiled a smaller, tighter smile, the smile I had taught myself, so I couldn't see the way my left eyetooth was crooked, edging toward my front tooth just a bit. I must have inherited that from my grandmother, although thank goodness it was just one tooth, and not all of them.

I took the cards back to Moo, who was sitting at the table drinking from a mug of black coffee. She unwrapped them and caressed the top card with her hand, then passed the deck to me. "Okay. Here we go. You shuffle, and then pick out five."

I did what she told me, handing the five cards to Moo and putting down the rest of the deck. She brushed crumbs off the tabletop with her sleeve, then laid the cards down, two side by side, then one a little higher, then another two side by side. "There. They're laid out to form the pages of a book, with the higher card in the middle signifying the binding that holds the pages together." She studied the cards, then picked up the first one.

"The Fool," she said.

"Great."

"Expect the unexpected. There are new opportunities and new horizons. A journey. One of self-discovery."

"Couldn't it be a real journey, Moo? One where I

actually get to go somewhere?" I would turn sixteen in less than two weeks, and I'd only been outside the city limits once. And that wasn't even further than a hundred miles.

"The Fool is a good card," Moo went on, running her finger up and down the side of the card. "It's related to the planet of independence and change — breaking away and making new starts."

"What's the next one, the five of ..." I looked at the picture, "swords, right?"

"That's right. Now, the five of swords is telling you that you have to stand and face up to problems. You can't run away from them."

Easy for the five of swords to say. Stand and face your problems, but it didn't say how to do it. "But the Fool said I was going on a journey. Now this card is saying I have to stay."

"Don't argue, just listen," Moo said. "You never argue with a diviner of the future; you know that. So you have to stay and fight, but be careful not to take on more than you can cope with." She sat quietly for a moment.

"Moo? The third card?" I glanced at the clock.

"We'll leave that one until last. Now, this fourth card is the Tower."

"It doesn't look good." In fact, it was sort of scary. A crumbling tower, with what looked like a bolt of lightning shooting into it. One guy sprawled out at the foot of the tower and another falling. I looked at Moo. Her eyes were narrowed.

"Well," she said, after taking a large swallow from her mug, "you can look at this card as positive or negative. It means that there are disruptions and setbacks, and some suffering. It causes concern, but it definitely means change. Things might happen suddenly — unexpectedly — and it seems like the world is collapsing. But," and she took another mouthful, "when the Tower falls, it's possible to rebuild, using the old bricks, plus some new ones, and create a different, but possibly better, building. Old forms collapse and new forms take their place."

She picked up the fifth card. "Here's the little nine of wands. And it's reversed."

"What does that mean?"

"When the nine of wands is reversed, you should take care of your health. Things going on around you might take their toll on you. So make sure you get enough rest."

Boring. "I have about two minutes before I have to leave, Moo. What's the last one? That queen."

Moo picked it up and held it in front of her face. "This is odd, Mercy. Very odd."

"Why?"

"It's the Queen of Cups."

"Why is that odd?"

"The card itself isn't odd, it's just that it keeps appearing. It's turned up in the two most recent readings I did for myself. And a few weeks ago, when Pearl let me do her last reading, she drew it. And now you. It's quite a coincidence, to keep drawing the same card out of a deck of seventy-eight cards."

I stood up, taking my jacket from the hook. "So what does the Queen of Cups stand for?"

"The Queen of Cups is a very strong and wise woman. She has a lot of foresight — she can see more than others. And not only does she see things, with this gift of vision, but she also acts, and makes her visions come true." She took another drink from her mug. "So there you go."

"Thanks, Moo."

"Remember that what I tell you isn't set in stone. There are a lot of ways to take the information. What you make of it, do with it, is the most important thing. Think about everything I've told you, and see how it can help you in your life."

"I know, I know." Moo said that, no matter what kind of reading she did.

She held her hand, palm up, on the tabletop. It was a silly ritual, the old gypsy cross-my-palm-with-silver routine. "For my payment, will you bring me a flower from work?"

"Yes, Moo. I'll try to bring you a flower."

Her lips turned up even further. "A rose. A pink one." She got up and poured herself a half cup of coffee, then reached into the cupboard over the stove. She pulled out the tall bottle of clear liquid, opened it, and streamed a generous splash into her coffee. "Just for my headache," she said, with a bit of a whine, as though I'd said anything about her drinking a coffee-gin cocktail for breakfast.

"I said I'll try to get you a flower. And I can't guarantee what it will be. It all depends." I watched her take a long drink of what was in her mug.

All that was left of my sweet taste of orange was a trace of acid on my tongue.

CHAPTER SIX

❦

I couldn't get a rose, but I brought a pink carnation home for Moo. It's not like I stole the flowers or anything. Vince says I can take any flowers that have bruised petals, or a bent stem, or anything like that. For the first little while I always showed him what I had; asked if it was okay.

"Mercy, I told you," he said. "How many times I gotta tell you? Take what you want. It's no big deal. I only throw them out anyway."

I'd been working here since before Christmas. As soon as we'd moved into this neighbourhood, I'd put applications in everywhere, but I never even got called in for an interview. I told myself it was because I was only fifteen.

I had really needed a job. We really needed me to get a job; to bring in some more money. And not just the kind of money from baby-sitting or delivering newspapers, like I'd done before. There was only B's rent money and whatever Moo made, but we could never depend from week to week on how much she'd work, or how she'd spend what money she did make.

Santa Marie Florist was on one of the main streets I had to walk down to get to school and back home again. The street had a few neat shops. There was a bookshop that buys and sells used books, and the owner would let me come in and browse for as long as I liked, even though I bought only the cheapest books every once in a while. Next door to the bookshop was a shop that sold clothes made in Peru, all stripes and woven fabrics; and next to that was an empty place with a FOR LEASE sign in the window. The bottom of the window was clear, but there was a beautiful stained-glass arch over the top. At a certain time in the late afternoon, the sun would shine through the stained glass and throw dancing arrows of colour on to the walls and floor, reminding me of a prism, or kaleidoscope. I loved to stop and watch the play of light and colour, imagining what the space could be someday. Beside that was a store that sold carpets from Turkey and Afghanistan, as well as gleaming and intricate brass candleholders and coffee mills, and even hanging bells; next to that was Santa Marie Florist.

Santa Marie had a big bowed-out front window, and the floral displays and arrangements sitting there were different each week. Every Monday I'd check out how the window display had been changed over the weekend, but I never paid any attention to who was inside the store. Then, on my way home one day in early December, as I stopped to pull my hat down lower over my ears, I saw a short man scurrying back and forth, unloading Christmas trees from the back of a truck sitting in the parking lot beside the store. The trees were all flat and stiff, and he was trying to get them stacked against one another inside a little fenced-in area of the parking lot. He'd keep turning around and looking toward the florist shop, like he was worried about something.

The next day he was out by the trees again, propping them up in little hills of snow. I watched as a woman walked into the shop. The man left the yard of trees, banging the gate behind him, and running inside, but this time throwing the same worried look to the trees.

I followed him into the store, partly out of curiosity, but mainly because my fingers and toes were freezing. The man was pointing to flowers that were behind the glass doors of the cabinets, and telling the woman what would look good with what. As I looked around, feeling the warmth of the store spread into my almost numb toes, I heard a little noise from behind the counter. It was a bit like chirping.

I glanced in that direction, and saw, not a bird, but a person. An old lady, really ancient and tiny and frail, sitting on a chair in the corner behind the counter. She was dressed in black — a black dress and a black shawl over her head and shoulders. Her skin reminded me of thin wrinkled paper, and her mouth was moving steadily and rhythmically. She could have been singing, or maybe even praying. When she saw me looking at her, she lifted one little hand and waved. I had been right about the praying; there was a delicate string of rosary beads wrapped around her fingers. She nodded and smiled, reminding me of a little cookie woman, with currant eyes in a tiny doughy face.

"I'll be right with you," the man had called to me. I looked at him, and he smiled. And even though there was no real resemblance, when he smiled, he somehow looked like the little woman in black.

"Okay," I said. I'd really come in only to get warm, and to look at the flowers, but when the man smiled, and his whole face changed, I started thinking about asking him for a job.

When the customer left, he came toward me. "What can I do for you?"

"I'm looking for a job," I said. "You look like you could use some help around here."

The man looked at my hair. At all my earrings. He looked down to my hands, half-covered by my sweater sleeves, pulled down through my coat sleeves. I folded my fingers in toward my palms, but I knew he'd already seen the chipped black nail polish.

"You want work?" he asked, frowning.

The little old woman called something to him in a foreign language. He answered her in the same language, then shook his head. "I don't think you'd like working here," he said. "You gotta know about plants, about flowers. About working with the public." His eyes flickered to the row of earrings up my ear.

"Yeah," I said. "Well, thanks anyway." At least he wasn't as rude to me as some people were, taking one look and then just shaking their heads when I asked if they needed part-time help.

I turned and left. As I went through the door, I heard the old lady chirping something again. I breathed deeply one more time; wanting to keep that clean, sweet smell with me for just a little longer.

I couldn't stop thinking about the florist shop. It was perfect — just a few blocks from home. And there was that smell. A few days later, as I got close to the store on my way home again, I saw him — the man — outside, shovelling snow from the sidewalk in front of the door. I glanced through the window. There was no one in the shop except for the little woman, swaying on the hard wooden chair, running the beads through her fingers.

"Hey," I said. I reached up and touched the ends of my hair, hoping the stiff, dyed texture would remind me I wasn't the same Mercy, the one in the park, screaming. I was older. Harder.

He stopped shovelling and leaned on the handle. A thin sheen of sweat glowed across his forehead, even though frosty air was streaming from his mouth.

"Listen. I really need a job. And I do know about plants, and flowers. And it doesn't look like you have any other help."

"You don't take 'no' for an answer?" he asked.

"Well, don't you? Need someone to work? I go to school, but I could work afterwards, or evenings. Weekends."

"Look. I told you before ..." He stopped as there was a loud rapping on the window. The old woman was there, knocking on the glass. When we both looked at her, she beckoned for us to come into the store.

The man shook his head at her. She nodded hers up and down, looking at me, shaking her finger at him, and calling through the glass in a scolding tone, in that same language I'd heard the first time.

"Okay, okay," he said. "Come on in for a minute." I waited while he banged the shovel once, hard, on the ground, to shake off the snow stuck on its sharp edge.

I followed him inside. The old woman stuck out her lips and nodded at me again. Then she spoke, clapping her hands together, once, when she was finished. She hobbled back to her chair behind the counter.

"You're not scared to ask for work, eh?" the man said. "You're not scared of hard work? And you know about plants?"

"No. No. And yes, a bit." I did know a little about flowers and plants; when I was younger one of our neighbours had her crowded apartment filled with all kinds of plants. I'd sometimes go in after school and the neighbour — I forget her name now, but she was quiet and had three cats and all these plants and blooming flowerpots — would give me something to eat and talk to me about her flowers.

Now the man wasn't saying anything, was just looking at me.

"I could fill something out. An application form or something." I wish he'd speak, stop looking at me like he was getting all the information he needed from what showed between the collar of my jacket and the top of my head.

"Okay. For now, have a look around. What's your name?"

"Mercy. Mercy Donnelly."

He held out one bare hand. "Vince Giovanni. You call me Vince." His hand closed around mine, and he shook it like he was priming a pump.

Vince pointed to a room behind the front counter where I could put my coat and hat. There was a tiny little fridge that fitted under the counter running along one short wall. The counter had a deep sink in it, and there was a coffee-maker filled with coffee that smelled fresh, and an open plastic container of cookies. I could see that they were the home-made kind, with chocolate chips and big chunks of walnuts. Saliva rushed into my mouth, and I had to swallow. As soon as I hung up my coat and turned around, there was that little woman, pushing the container at me. I took a cookie and bit into it. It was soft and chewy, wonderful. I had this sudden feeling of nostalgia — that sad longing for something good that doesn't exist anymore. Even a whiff of baking from the home economics room at school does it to me now.

"Thank you," I said, chewing. There was a radio with a tape deck on the counter, the sound of opera pouring from it. A crying, begging, Italian voice. Of course Giovanni is an Italian name. That's what Vince and the old woman had been speaking. She put one gnarled hand in the air, her fingers spread, and rocked her hand, like a boat on calm water, to the music.

Vince came in. "Okay, Mercy, come into the cooler. We'll see what you really know."

I followed him through the front area, with the counter and cash register and glass-fronted cabinets holding flower arrangements and big containers of cut flowers, into another room with a sliding glass door. There were potted plants lined up on shelves, and more huge containers of flowers.

I hoped I could impress him, just a little. I started naming what I saw. "Those are roses, and those are daisies." I kept on, surprising even myself. I knew quite a few. "And that plant is an ivy, and that's a spider plant. Pearl — that's my mother — she had a couple of spider plants once. Those two are types of ferns ..."

"You call your mother Pearl?"

"Yes."

"How come you do that?"

I shrugged. "I just always have. I don't really know. I guess she must have told me to, when I was little."

"You call your father his first name, too?"

"No. I live with my mother and Moo. My aunt."

Vince shook his head. "No," he said. "It's not right. You have one mother in this life. You should treat her with respect. You should call her Mom, Mother, Mommy, Mama — something sweet and nice. And Moo. What kind of name is that?"

I got an uncomfortable feeling. What did my home life have to do with wanting a job wrapping up flowers for people? "Her name is actually Maureen. When I was starting to talk, I couldn't say Maureen, so I just said Moo."

"At least you say Auntie Moo?" he asked, a hopeful look on his face.

"No. Just Moo. That's a cactus, obviously." I tried to change the subject. "And all these small ones here, on this stand, they're African violets, right? I know they like late afternoon sun. And you can't get water on their leaves, or it makes spots."

"Names are important. Hey, Mama," he said, as

the woman came into the cooler. She was eating one of the cookies .

"That's my mama, and I call her Mama." His eyes were level with mine. "Her name is Mrs Giovanni, but nobody calls her that. The neighbourhood kids, they started calling her Mama Gio. She likes it."

Obviously this guy had a hang-up with names.

I looked at the old lady. "Hi, Mama Gio."

She made a sound that was a bit like giggling.

"This is Mercy, Mama. Mercy." He said something in Italian, then told me, "I had another kid here, until last month, but she quit. I got my cousin Theresa coming in part-time, too, but she's pretty busy. I can't rely on her. And my mama, her legs are bad now. She can't stand for long." He looked at her and nodded. "So now she's happy. I told her okay, okay, we'll give you a trial run for a few weeks. See if you work out."

I realized I had the job. At least for now.

Later, Vince showed me how to work the cash register, and how to pull paper off the big roll and lay flowers in the middle. Also to put in a little packet of white flower preserver, and tell people they should cut the stems at an angle when they got the flowers home — not with scissors, because that can seal the stem shut so the water can't get in, but with a sharp knife, and preferably under running water. And to remind them that the water should be lukewarm, not cold. He also told me that he was born in Italy, in the town of Santa Marie near Naples, and that's why he'd named the store Santa

Marie. That he came to Canada with his family when he was still a boy.

"Just a kid. I was a kid, but I already knew how to work like a man. All my life, working for other people, I dreamed of my own business. And I made my dream come true."

It was impossible to tell Vince's age; in some ways he looked old, bent over the flowers, his face lined and eyelids puckered and heavy over his narrow eyes, which were such a deep brown that they were almost black. Then he'd laugh when he was showing me something, and run his fingers through his thick, curly black and grey hair, and I'd think I was wrong; he wasn't that old after all. When I saw him walking out into the lot to help someone with a Christmas tree, the space between his legs made a bowed-out O, an oval, like you'd see in a cartoon drawing of a cowboy. His arms seemed too long for his body, and bulged with muscles. His hands hung from his hairy wrists like great creatures from the sea, red and gnarled and crisscrossed with scars, like a map that's been opened and folded too many times.

But even on that first day, I saw that his hands could touch a rose so softly that it wouldn't even tremble.

CHAPTER SEVEN

❦

At first I thought Andrea was just hanging around me because I was new. She was in my art class as well as English. I gave her a few days, sure she'd back off when I hardly answered her. After all, she had other friends. Three girls — Miki, Elsbeth, and Kiera. She was with them most of the time. She realized early on that I didn't like to be with the whole group; I would sit with her if she was alone, but if the four of them were together, I pretended I didn't see them.

Miki, Elsbeth, Kiera — and Andrea — were the girls that didn't fit anywhere. They weren't bouncy and confident, wearing the clothes you see in all those teen fashion magazines, so they didn't get to hang out with Starr and her crowd. They weren't on any of the school sports teams; they weren't the academics, and they weren't into drama or music. They weren't team players, but they weren't loners.

I didn't fit anywhere either, but I had always told myself I liked it that way. It seemed like too much work to have a friend.

"You seem like you don't even want to have friends," Andrea had said to me, a few weeks after the first time she'd talked to me.

"I've done alright without them so far," I said, as we walked down the hall toward the art room.

"But it's more fun."

"What is?"

Andrea had shrugged. "I don't know. Everything. It's more fun to do stuff with other people. Tell them your secrets. Talk about stuff that's important to you."

I hadn't said anything.

"I mean, secrets aren't as scary when you tell someone."

I'd never come across anyone like Andrea at my other schools. She didn't get tired of saying "hi" to me in the halls, or waving for me to join her in the cafeteria, or trying to get a seat near me in English or art. I have to give her credit. She was the first person who didn't take it personally if I didn't feel like talking. She'd make up for my silences, rattling away without asking anything, just telling. The majority of what she talked about had to do with school — gossip about kids, stories about what teachers had done or not done, and homework. Safe territory for me, and, I started to realize, for her.

"Tell me something, Andrea," I said, later, as we were working at the big tables in the light-filled art room. We could pick what we wanted to make for a Christmas project. Andrea was cutting out pictures from magazines and old Christmas cards, and gluing them on a wooden block. Then she would varnish over it all. Découpage, our art teacher, Mr Lindstrom, called it. I was working with a lump of soft clay, trying to shape it into a small bowl, without much success.

"Yeah?"

"Why did you talk to me, that first day of school, when we were coming out of English?"

Andrea picked up the glue bottle. "Why did I talk to you?"

"Yeah. I just wondered." I had my head down, trying to curl the long strips of smooth clay so they'd stay together.

"Well, actually, it was what you were writing, during class." She stopped, and I looked over at her.

"What I was writing?"

"It was a bunch of sentences, like a poem. I was sitting behind you, and I could see it. I read it. Your binder was open, right in my line of vision. I wasn't spying or anything," she added. "The poem about some cold grey stones, and the sea, and ships going by. And I remember that I really loved the last two lines. Something about a vanished hand. A voice that didn't speak."

"'But O, for the touch of a vanished hand, And the sound of a voice that is still.' That one?"

"Yeah."

I frowned. "And? Why did reading that over my shoulder make you talk to me?"

Andrea lowered her head and I saw the tip of her tongue come out and lick her top lip. "It was how I feel. About my dad."

I waited.

"He and my mom split up last year, and he moved to British Columbia. I really miss him. When I read what you wrote about that — the vanished hand, and the silenced voice — it made me feel sad. But good, in another way. I thought, well, maybe I wasn't the only one sitting in English, not listening, missing someone. I thought maybe you were, too. Because you were writing about missing someone that you love."

"That was from a poem by Tennyson. It's called 'Break, Break, Break.'"

"Oh. You didn't make it up?"

"Andrea. Alfred, Lord Tennyson is only one of the great classic poets. As if I could write like that!"

Andrea raised her eyebrows. "Well, you *look* like the kind of person who would write poetry. Dark, mysterious. Like you've got all kinds of secrets."

"Starr thinks I look like one of Macbeth's witches. Not that I care," I added.

"No. How could you look like a witch? You have a totally unbelievable face. Your eyes are such a strange colour — but strange in a good way. Sort of yellowy-brown, with flecks of gold in them. And all those tiny freckles over your nose are like matching flecks of gold on your skin." She stopped, and made a goofy face, like she was embarrassed for saying those things to me. "Although I'd try to do something about that wart on the end of your nose," she said, with a sudden grin.

I picked up a hunk of clay and smeared it on Andrea's cheek. A tiny shriek escaped from between her lips.

"Ladies, ladies," Mr Lindstrom called out. "A little decorum, please."

"Découpage, decorum," Andrea muttered, wiping her cheek with her hand. "Why does he have to use words we don't understand?"

"It means to act in a proper manner. Decorum," I

said. Andrea shook her head. "I don't know who's worse. You or long-winded Lindstrom."

"You may mean loquacious Lindstrom," I told her. "A tendency toward continuous talking. Although, actually, that suits you, my dear. Mr Lindstrom doesn't say that much, but what he does say leans toward ostentation."

"Shut up," Andrea said, pushing against my shoulder with her own. "You're always doing that. When anyone else is around, you don't say anything. But when it's just you and me, you use that big fancy language."

"That big fancy language, as you call it, is my true language. The language of my soul. My poetic soul, I should add."

"I said shut *up,*" Andrea said, her voice rising to a near shriek on the last word.

"One more sound, and detention for both of you," Mr Lindstrom yelled across the room.

"Was that simple enough for you, or shall I translate?" I whispered to Andrea.

You die, Andrea spelled out with her fingernail into my lump of unused clay.

I kept working my clay, but thought about Andrea telling me I had an unbelievable face. Nobody'd ever said anything like that to me before.

After Andrea first told me about her father, it was like she couldn't stop talking about him. "He was so much fun," she would go on. "He and I did all these neat things together."

I'd just nod, or make some noise in my throat. She

didn't seem to notice that I was bored stiff. One time over lunch in the school cafeteria, she was telling me about some incredibly wonderful vacation that sounded incredibly dull. How she and her dad had gone bungee jumping, while her mom and older sister stood on the ground with the video camera. There was more, but I'd stopped listening, and was dragging one of my fries back and forth through the congealing gravy on my plate.

"Do you? Mercy!" She'd shaken my arm.

"What?"

"I asked you a question. If you ever see your dad. You've never said anything about him."

"No. He left before I was born," I said.

"Oh. I'm really sorry."

I looked at her. "Why? I'm not. I don't know what I'm missing, so I don't miss him."

"Does he write, or anything?"

I shook my head.

"What was his name?"

She just wouldn't give up. "Jimbo," I said. As soon as I said it, I realized what a stupid name it was. I'd never said it out loud. The only reason I knew it was Jimbo was from the back of an old picture of him and my mom — grinning, sitting together on a mean-looking motorcycle. "Me and Jimbo on his Harley Davidson," it said. Not James, or Jamie, Jim, or even Jimmy. I had a father somewhere out there named Jimbo. And from what I can tell, after he left Pearl (and me, although I wasn't a person to him), my mother swore she'd never take another chance.

"And your mom never got married again or anything?"

"Nope."

"Does she have a boyfriend?"

Pearl had never had a boyfriend. Not that I knew about, anyway. But Moo — that was a whole other story. She had two ex-husbands, neither of whom I could remember very clearly. But I had seen too many of her jerky boyfriends: there were the ones who borrowed money, but forgot to mention they'd lost their jobs, so couldn't pay it back; the ones who told her they wanted to marry her, but forgot to mention that they were married, or at least involved with someone else; and the ones who promised they'd always stay, but forgot to mention they were just on their way through town. Until B.

B's fingers were hard, calloused from all the outside work he did. They had felt like sandpaper on my cheek.

"What's wrong, Mercy? You're acting all weird."

"No. My mother doesn't have a boyfriend." I realized I was standing and, when I went to sit down again, I knocked against the edge of my plate so that the last of my fries scattered on to the floor. A big blob of beige gravy ran down my skirt. I swiped it off with a paper napkin. "I have to go to class."

"But it's not even close to one o'clock yet. And you didn't finish your lunch."

I hadn't answered, just left the table, leaving Andrea sitting there with that big-eyed look.

I had realized that B had been gone for six months. Seven or eight, that's what he'd said. "See you in seven months, eight, tops." I realized, at that moment, that I was just like my mother, and like my aunt. I was pretending that it wasn't going to happen, that he wasn't going to be back, and that I didn't have to figure out a way to tell someone what I was so afraid of.

I'd been trying not to think about it while time was running out. And instead of it getting easier to talk to Moo or Pearl, it was even harder.

❦

I think one of my last real conversations with Pearl had been just before Christmas.

"How's your new school?" she'd asked.

I'd been there for two months.

"It's alright."

"Are the kids nice?"

Nice? "Not really," I answered. "A few are okay. There's one girl that I hang around with — Andrea. But that's about it." I dumped some Cheerios into a bowl, and took the carton of milk out of the fridge. "This is skimmed," I said, holding it up. "Why did Moo buy this? I hate skimmed milk."

"Mercy?"

I poured the milk over the cereal. "Yeah?"

"You shouldn't dye your hair like that."

I didn't say anything.

"It's so, well, black. And maybe you should wear something else. Black can turn people off. Maybe you're sending a message. Do you know what I mean?"

"Of course I'm sending a message, Pearl. Do you think I'm stupid or something?" I stuck the milk back in the fridge and took a spoon from the sink. It didn't look dirty. I smelled it, but there was only a faint scent of tea along with the stronger one of stainless steel. "I'm sending a message that says I like black." I carried my bowl into the living room and sat down on the couch. Pearl followed me, but didn't come into the room. She stood in the doorway, watching me eat.

I kept on spooning up the little o's and chewing. The watery milk made them taste like cardboard. "What?" I finally said to her, when there was only a splash of liquid left in the bowl.

She lifted her shoulders in a half shrug. Her hair stuck up in tufts on the top of her head, and was flattened on one side, where she'd been lying on it. She reminded me of a baby bird whose feathers aren't grown in yet, whose head seems too big for its body, all scraggy and half-naked, even though Pearl was bundled in layers of clothes. Over a thick navy turtleneck sweater she wore a beige cardigan, with the top and the bottom buttons missing. But it wasn't buttoned up anyway; Pearl had it wrapped around her with her own arms, hugging herself, as if she was trying to keep warm, or keep something inside.

"So that's it?" I asked. "No more pearls of wisdom?" I smiled at my own joke, but my mother didn't seem to get it. "No more lectures on how to make friends?"

She still hadn't moved.

"Well, thank you very much, Pearl." Mother-of-Pearl, a pearl of a mother — take your pick. "You're a wellspring of advice." I lifted the bowl and drank from it. The milk tasted watery, sad and transparent, like it was fake — only pretending to be milk.

CHAPTER EIGHT

❦

Andrea keeps asking me over to her place, but I don't go very often, for two reasons. One is that I work a lot after school, and another is because if I keep on going to her house, I'll have to invite her to mine sometime.

She asked me again today, shifting her books to her other arm as we went toward our lockers after school. "Walk home with me, okay? You could stay for supper; my mom wouldn't mind."

"Can't." I stopped at my locker and started dialling the combination of my lock.

"How come?"

I pulled down on the lock; it didn't open. "Damn," I said, under my breath, and started dialling again. "I'm ... working.

"Mercy! You're *always* working. How can you stand it? You never have any fun."

I gave another tug. The lock clicked open and I swung the locker door wide. Andrea was pretty smart about a lot of things. I was surprised she hadn't figured out that I was working for the money. Shoving my books inside, I thought about being there, at Santa Marie, and realized it was the one place I really wanted to be. It wasn't just the money. It was the only place I felt calm: like nothing could hurt me; like I didn't have to worry about anything or anyone. For the first month I'd tiptoed around, making sure I did everything perfectly, so Vince would have no reason to tell me it wouldn't work out. I even stopped wearing black nail polish after a customer complained to him about it, and Vince told me you have to look clean, if nothing else, when you deal with the public. He'd said "if nothing else" with a shake of his head, looking at my hair, but that was all.

"I'd hate working so much," Andrea said. "Hey, don't look over there. It's Starr. She and Monique are watching us."

I turned in the direction Andrea was facing.

"Mercy," Andrea hissed. "I said, 'Don't look.' "

I waited just long enough to see Starr's head lean toward Monique's, and then two pairs of eyes stare at me, and a hand come up to each face to catch the whispers.

"I don't know which one of them I hate the most," Andrea said. "Stop looking at them."

"As if I care what they think about me," I said to Andrea, closing my locker door hard enough to let the hollow, tinny slam reach all the way down the hall to hit Starr and Monique.

The door was locked, and the blind on the window in the upper part of the door pulled down. I knocked once, then again, harder; then moved over and looked through the almost closed wooden shutters of the window. I could see the tables and chairs and counter, with its cappuccino maker and long row of glass jars holding various coloured tea leaves. The room looked like it was made up of long, horizontal pieces.

I caught a swish of softly coloured fabric just disappearing behind a high curtained screen — fruit colours of strawberry and honeydew and lemon — out of place in the bright hardness inside the restaurant, out of place in the grey slush outside on the street.

"Moo!" I called, banging on the window with my fist. "Out here. Moo!"

The colours came into view again; Moo's slow, plodding movements across the room. When she swept open the door, her mouth opened wide. "Mercy!" she said. "What are you doing here?"

"Don't you remember?" I took a breath, blew it out, and took another. Moo's smile faded just the slightest. "You don't, do you? Last night you asked if I could come and help you open at ten thirty this morning, because Mr and Mrs Henkel are away at some special church thing for the day. And because of your hand. You said you couldn't do much with it. Then you got up and left while I was still asleep."

Moo looked down at her right hand, a piece of fraying gauze wrapped round and round and tied on the side with two torn strips of the same gauze. She turned her hand over and looked at the palm.

"Is that blood?" There was a faint brown-red stain along one side of the gauze.

"I don't think so," she answered. She put her hand to her nose and sniffed. "Nope. Country Cranberry tea. I made some for myself earlier."

I pushed past her, raised the blind, and folded the shutters back so that light flooded into the room.

"What do you have left to do? Customers might be in anytime."

Moo stood there, swaying slightly. Her turban matched her caftan. She wore caftans a lot. Moo-moos, I used to call them, to bug her. She said the outfits made her look more authentic for her fortune-teller role. I knew she wore the caftans because they were comfortable, and the turbans so she didn't have to worry about her hair. Her hair was pale brown, with white strands here and there. It was thin and straight. She usually pulled it back into a short ponytail at the back of her neck if she wasn't wearing a turban.

"Let me think. Oh, vacuum. I didn't vacuum." She looked down at the carpet, as if it might somehow communicate this truth with her. "And I couldn't wipe stuff up very well. Because I couldn't get this wet." She held up her hand again.

"Did you get the money from the safe and put it in the cash register? Start the coffee? Fill the big kettle?"

Moo blinked once, then nodded.

I went to the back room and dragged out the vacuum. Moo was sitting at the table in the corner, just sitting there, looking at her bandaged hand.

"When can you take that off?" I asked. Two days ago Moo had sliced into the palm of her hand while she was cutting a bagel.

"Probably another day or so. It wasn't all that deep, but the doctor said to make sure the stitches were dissolved." She kept looking at it. "Want to know something?"

I didn't answer. Moo always said that — want to

know something? — and then told you whether you wanted to know or not.

"I just realized, they'll never be the same again."

I pushed the plug into the wall socket and straightened up. "What won't?"

"My lines. Heart and head. I missed my life line, but the other two were cut through. That changes my palm."

I stepped on the switch, and the vacuum roared. I started pushing the heavy old machine over the crumbs and sandy dirt that littered the carpet. How could my aunt's head and heart be affected any more than they already were? But I could see why she was concerned. After all, hands were part of her job, at this shabby little place that offered coffee and tea and sandwiches, and slices of quiche, or squares of lasagne.

Of course, Moo always pretended that she had nothing to do with that part of the job. She was there to take people behind the little curtained-off area in the corner, and tell their futures.

This was like a dim, ugly version of the shop she and my mother had planned to own someday.

The first customers didn't come in until almost noon: two women, who bought coffee and sat by the front windows and talked. It got busier after that, a small but steady procession of people coming in for coffee or tea or a sandwich. I did the food, and after Moo spilled the first two cups of coffee she tried to carry, I served that, too.

Moo had only one reading — a regular that comes

in every Sunday afternoon to have Moo read her tea leaves and tell her what to expect for the following week.

"It's a good thing Vince didn't need me today," I told Moo, when we were finally alone. She was sitting by the window, looking out and drinking from a teacup.

"And it's a good thing Mr or Mrs Henkel didn't see you like this. You'll get fired, Moo. And then what? Even with my salary, we've hardly got enough money."

She put her cup down. "You want to know something, Mercy? Business hasn't been good. Not good at all."

I cleaned out the sink. "There have been a lot of customers today; I thought it was really busy for a Sunday."

"No." Moo shook her head and wiped at her eyes. "I meant my business. The readings. They've really tapered off."

"Oh."

"How are we ever going to start Donnelly's Desserts if I can't bring in enough steady customers, Mercy?" She sniffed. Moo cried really easily.

Pearl had written it on paper more times than I could count: DONNELLY'S DESSERTS, in big letters, and then, in smaller letters underneath: MAUREEN GRAPKO, SEER.

"I don't know, Moo," I said. Moo still hadn't given up the dream, although it had never seemed to mean as much to her as it had to my mother. Like men, Moo always had another dream around the corner.

The door opened, and a cold blast of air billowed around my ankles.

"I'll serve them," Moo said, and I kept on at the sink. It wasn't until Moo said, "What can I get you? And would you be interested in having me tell your fortunes? Pretty girls like you must have all kinds of things in store," that I turned around.

Starr and Monique were staring at Moo, and in that instant I saw my aunt as they must have — her caftan and turban, her huge bulk, the cup in her hand slopping liquid over one side. I saw them look at each other, and saw the slow smiles start on their mouths.

"Well, girls? Pick your table. Anywhere you'd like to sit."

"We're not staying," Monique said. Her voice was loud and bossy.

"Yeah. We just came in to get some hot chocolate, to take out." Starr started walking toward the counter. "You have hot chocolate, don't you?" At the last word, she saw me. She stopped, and I could just picture her little brain clicking away. Another small smile. She tried to stop it, and put on an expression of friendly surprise. "Don't you go to my school?"

"Hot chocolate? Is that what you want?" I took two Styrofoam cups from under the counter.

"So you work here?" Starr said. She looked around. "What a ... cute little place."

I started filling the cups from the hot chocolate machine.

Moo rustled up behind them. "Are these your friends, dear? I'm her aunt."

No, I thought. *Don't let this be happening.*

"Well," Monique said, "I think she goes to our school."

"Yeah," Starr added. "And her name is, um, something that starts with an M..."

"Morticia," Monique said, too softly for Moo to hear. "Like in the Addams family." Her eyes slyly found mine. I stared back at her.

Moo moved beside me. "Yes. It's Mercy. And she doesn't work here. She's just helping me out. I don't really work here, either." She laughed, and I saw Starr and Monique lean back. I could smell it, too, the reek of alcohol from Moo's breath, even though I hadn't noticed it before. "I mean, I do, but not serving. I'm not a waitress. I'm a teller of the future. But the owner is away, and I hurt my —"

Starr interrupted. "How much is that?" she asked me, as I set the cups on the counter in front of her.

"One fifty each."

Moo just wouldn't stop. "Isn't this nice? Mercy doesn't know too many people because we only moved here a while ago. Right, Mercy? Mercy, do you know that these girls go to your school?"

"Yeah," I said, looking at the bit of foamy chocolate bubbling up through the openings on the lids I'd pushed down on top of the cups.

"Did I hear you say you actually ... could tell fortunes?" Starr's phoney interested voice matched her smile. She put three dollars on the counter.

Could this please end? Now?

"Yes," Moo said. "I can read your palm, or, if you have a cup of tea, I'll read the leaves. I do tarot cards, too."

"How much do you charge?" This time it was Monique.

"Well, my usual fee is ten dollars. That's for a fifteen minute reading. But I could make an exception. For friends of Mercy's."

Starr and Monique looked at me again. "Maybe some other time," Starr said. "We don't have time right now. We're on our way somewhere. To another friend's house."

Moo looked at me. "You don't have to stay, honey. You go on with the girls. I can close up. It's almost closing time, isn't it?"

Please, Moo, just shut up. Can't you see anything? Anything at all? If you can see the future, why can't you see what's happening right now? This is the present, Moo — my present — and thanks to you, and to Pearl, it stinks.

"Oh, we wouldn't want to stop Mercy from doing her job," Monique said. "Hurry up, Starr. We can't be late. Don't work too hard, you two." She covered her mouth with one hand, pretending to clear her throat, but I heard the word she said. "Loser."

When they were gone, Moo shook her head at me. "You should have gone with them, Mercy. You should be out with your friends more."

"My friends? My friends?" I snorted. "You think those girls are my friends? You didn't see how they were treating me? Us? We're just a joke to them, Moo. You and me, two big jokes."

I walked to the door and locked it, then stood looking out the glass on the door. "That's us, Moo. You and me, two big jokes. Ha, ha, ha. Why aren't you laughing?" But I wasn't really saying it to Moo.

It was my own form I could see, reflecting back at me in the glass — my hair a dark, stiff mass, my face a pale, featureless oval.

I pulled the blind down so hard that there was a frenzied whirring from the roller.

CHAPTER NINE

"How are we doing?" Mr Lindstrom asked, then coughed.

"Fine," I said. The drama club needed masks for one of the scenes of the upcoming production. Mr Lindstrom had volunteered his grade ten art class to make them.

I took another strip of newspaper from the wet pulpy mess in the bowl in front of me, and smoothed it on to the shape growing over the round balloon.

The dry cough again. Mr Lindstrom had sagging, discoloured bags under his eyes. Everything on his face was pulled down by lines — his eyes, his nose, his mouth. He kept standing beside me, watching.

I concentrated on the next layer. The soaked newspaper was making my fingers black.

I saw Mr Lindstrom's feet take a step forward, then stop. "Inventive. It will be interesting to see when it's painted. What colours do you plan to use?"

I looked up, but it hurt to look at that bruised, purplish flesh around his eyes. I shifted my gaze to his shoulder.

"Eggplant," I said. *Aubergine.*

But I didn't paint it dark purple. The next art class, when all the papier mâché had dried, I painted it yellow, bright yellow. Around the eyeholes I painted a fine border of rich mossy green, ending at the outside corner of each eve with masses of tiny lines that curled up to create a swirl of tendrils.

There was a slight bump that could fit over my nose. The mouth was just a long slice above the chin. Unless you looked closely, you could hardly see it.

When I got home, Pearl and Moo were sitting at the table, Moo looking at her half-full glass, and Pearl looking at her hands on the grey plastic tabletop. Voices sounded from the living room — the television.

"What's going on?" I asked. I don't know why I asked; it was quite a normal scene in our house. But there was something else, something I couldn't quite catch — like I just missed the last few words in a whispered conversation, or someone quietly slipped out the back door. I put my jacket and my backpack on the high stack of old newspapers that was piled on the floor under the coats. It kept getting higher. Each week Mrs Henkel let Moo bring home all the papers she kept for her customers to read while they were having their morning coffee. I guess Moo thought she'd get around to reading them all someday.

"What's happening?" I asked again. And again, neither of them answered. I sat down on the chair between them and put my hands on the top of the table, my fingers spread wide.

Pearl's eyes moved from the plastic to my right hand, close to hers on the table, as if she were concentrating on it. Then, from the living room, came a BBC voice — one of those low, but carrying, British accents. "And here, only an inch below the surface of the earth, is where the miracle occurs." In the silence that followed, I felt like we were all waiting, straining our ears for something, perhaps the miracle, to make itself known.

But when only dark, damp, rhythmic sounds, which could have been a train underwater, or possibly the chewing of thousands of tiny insect mandibles, wafted through the doorway, Pearl said, "Happening? What do you mean?" And she hoisted herself — if you can weigh about ninety pounds and still hoist, but she gave the impression that her body weighed as much as Moo's — from her chair and walked out of the kitchen, stopping for about three seconds in the doorway, as if she really didn't want to leave.

But she did, and I heard her snap off the television, then the door to her bedroom closed with a quiet click.

Moo stood and took another gulp of her drink. She started rummaging through a drawer with one hand; her glass, held in the other, raining colourless lethal droplets on to the spoons and forks. She muttered as she dug and rattled, finally holding up a vegetable peeler in a sort of defeated way, as if now that she'd found it, it wasn't what she wanted.

"Get out some plates, Mercy," Moo said, still not turning to face me, "and in a few minutes check on the meat loaf in the oven. I found a recipe in the newspaper. It called for salsa, but we didn't have any, so I used a can of tomato soup. I don't know if it will be alright. And get that bowl of pudding from the fridge. I made pudding this afternoon. Chocolate."

"Moo?" I said. Moo was never this organized about supper, or anything. But she ignored me, pausing to drain her glass, then turned toward the counter and started in on the three big potatoes sitting by the sink, each scrape, scrape, scrape of the peeler quick and final.

"There was a rerun of *Mary Tyler Moore* on this afternoon," she said. "I love those old shows. Want to know something? When I was younger, people used to tell me I looked like her. Mary Tyler Moore. I was a lot slimmer back then. Had a good figure."

I looked at her broad back and the flesh of her heavy upper arm jiggling as she worked the peeler. Her voice was different, not slow and slurred like it often was by the end of the day, and not the deep, serious tone she used in her tarot-card readings. It was a higher voice, breathier, like she had just run up the basement stairs after making some startling discovery in a cobwebby corner.

"I thought I'd try to make a nice supper tonight. Sort of a celebration."

I set the table. The heavy clink of dishes and glasses, the clatter of cutlery, the opening and closing of the fridge door, cupboard doors — the opening and closing, opening and closing — slammed through the kitchen. It was like the noise was trying to make up for what wasn't being said. The table was set, and as I bent over to check on the meat loaf, it hit me.

I closed the oven door and straightened up, turning

my back on the stove. "What are we celebrating, Moo?" But I realized that I knew the answer. I'd known it from the moment I walked in the door, and saw my mother and aunt sitting at the table. I knew what it meant, but I couldn't let myself think about it.

Moo didn't turn around, and at that moment I heard my mother's voice. "Mercy." Pearl's voice had the same high, breathy sound as Moo's. Funny, because normally they didn't sound one bit alike. "Would you come here?"

"Coming," I called, trying to keep that same awful, fake sound out of my own voice. Maybe it was contagious — the voice thing. "I'm coming," I said again, not leaving my spot, feeling the warmth of the stove heating the backs of my legs, feeling a strangely familiar and yet warning beat at the edge of my mind; seeing, out of the corner of my eye, that Moo had stopped peeling, her arm up in front of her, the peeler clenched in one fist, the half-stripped potato in the other. Her bulk was still, as if suspended in the elastic time of a moment's bad dream. Except that it was my bad dream, coming true. Not hers.

B was coming back. That's why she wanted to celebrate.

CHAPTER TEN

❦

Pearl's room had a smell — something I recognized, but that didn't seem right here. It wasn't just the smell of cigarette smoke; Pearl used to smoke a lot, but now she can't afford it, so she makes a pack last almost two weeks. I inhaled again, and placed the smell. Sometimes plants got too big for their containers, and Vince or I would transplant them. Afterwards one of my jobs was to clean out the old terracotta pots to use again. The soil was all used up; even with proper watering and regular feeding to keep the plant healthy, the soil had had it. It had lost its good clean scent, and now there was only an earthy, tired-out smell. Not bad, but not good.

"Do you want these?" Pearl asked. She was holding out a ring, a small gold ring with a solitaire diamond, and a string of shiny brown beads on a silver chain.

I looked at them, lying in her hand. "Your engagement ring? And the necklace ... you said your mom sent it to you, for your high school graduation." I shook my head. "You keep them. I don't want them. Is it him? Is he ... back?"

Pearl looked down at the jewellery. "I won't wear them again.

I watched her, and did this thing with my eyes

that I can do. If I think about it really hard, I can block out everything except what I'm looking at. Almost like what they call tunnel vision, except that's an involuntary sight problem. It's as if you can see only straight ahead, down a long tube. I don't have the real tunnel vision, but I can make myself see only the thing right in front of me, blocking out everything else. And I can do it whenever I want, as long as I concentrate, and then I blink and the rest of the world fills in again. So now I concentrated, and soon all I could see was Pearl's head, and a tiny background of faded flowery wallpaper behind her, as if she were a picture in a frame.

It feels like I'm stopping time when I do it. And if I could stop this moment, then I wouldn't have to hear the thing I was most afraid of hearing.

After a minute Pearl moved; she ran her fingers through her hair. We used to have the same kind of hair, thick and glossy, the identical red-gold. Pearl cut hers really short a few months ago, and now it seems to have lost its shine, and the colour looks somehow faded. And since I started dyeing mine, it's not shiny anymore. It's dull and stiff, not inviting anyone to touch it. The way I want it.

Thinking about why I cut and dyed my hair made me lose my concentration, and I blinked. The rest of the room swam into focus. "I don't want your jewellery," I said. "It doesn't mean anything to me."

Pearl held the ring up. "An engagement ring." The one tiny diamond winked at me. "That's it, Merce. No wedding ring. Just an engagement ring. That's all I got out of the deal."

Her eyes seemed to be set back further in her head than I remembered. "And me," I said. "You got me out of that deal."

She held up the beads. "And a necklace from a mother, who ..."

I waited. "Who what, Pearl? What about Grandma?" The only other picture I had seen of my grandmother, apart from the one on Moo's dresser, was in an old photo album on the top of Moo's closet shelf. In this picture, she was older, and she wasn't smiling. She was clenching four-year-old Maureen's hand, and had baby Pearl stiffly perched on her hip.

Moo or Pearl would never say much about her, although I knew she sent us a Christmas card each year, and I think Moo wrote to her sometimes. Once, when I asked Pearl what kind of mother Grandma was, Pearl's lip had curled up, but it wasn't a smile.

"An absent one," she'd said, and that was all.

They both did talk about their father, my grandfather. But he'd died when I was a baby. There were even some pictures of him holding me on his lap. But none of me and my grandmother. And just the one of my parents on the motorcycle. Moo had quite a few of herself and the men who'd come and gone in her life. But our family album was definitely lacking.

Pearl looked down at her hand again — the one holding the jewellery — and then she closed it, making a tight fist over the ring and necklace. "So you don't want them?"

"No." I fought to keep my voice level. "Why are you trying to give them to me?"

She didn't move.

"Pearl. Never mind those things. Is Barry coming back?"

But she didn't answer my question. She opened the top drawer of her dresser and tossed the ring and necklace in, then slid the drawer shut with a bang. She rubbed her hands down the front of her sweatshirt, as if they were dirty. Then she lay down on her bed, her back toward me.

I looked at the thin curved S of her spine.

"Can you go? I'm a little tired right now," she said.

"Pearl." I pushed her shoulder. She didn't respond. "Pearl," I said louder. "Turn over and look at me. Talk to me. I asked you a question. I asked you if Barry was coming back. But it's too soon. Is he?"

When she still didn't move, the quiet rage that had been slowly filling up in me exploded out of my mouth.

"What's wrong with you?" I yelled. "Don't you care about me? You're making my life hell. You and Moo. Don't you realize what's happening here?"

B is back, B is back, B is back, kept up a steady drumming beneath my tongue.

"I have this friend, Andrea, but I don't really want to be friends with her because then she'll have to come here and see how I live. I have a job where I bring home more money than Moo, and at least we've got food in the cupboards all the time now. And I like working there. They're nice to me. I was just starting to feel like maybe, maybe, for once in my life, things might be okay. And now this."

I wasn't saying it, wasn't saying *and now B, B*

will come in and destroy me, destroy my life, and nobody will help me, because you're both too weak and useless. But instead, I said, "Come on! Get up! Do something. Be something. Be a mother, for once in your life! Do just one little thing to show me you care about me, that you care what happens to me!" I was actually screaming in the small, warm room. Like Pearl's had been, my hands were curled into tight fists. I didn't want to touch her again; I was afraid that if I did, I might start hitting at her, slapping with open hands, the way a small child slaps out at anyone nearby during a tantrum.

When I stopped, everything grew very calm; Pearl was even more still, except for a pulse beating in the side of her neck.

"Pearl," I said, not yelling anymore.

All that came from Pearl was a little whooshing whisper, like the sound when you squeeze the last bit of air out of a plastic bag. The pulse in her neck beat along with my own heart.

I heard a snuffle outside the open door. Moo was standing there, her hands at her throat. Tears streamed from her eyes. I looked back at Pearl, and saw that the pulse was even slower. I knew she wouldn't say anything.

"Now my celebration supper is ruined," Moo said to me, sniffling. "Isn't it? Nobody's going to eat it. Not that Pearl would have anyway. And now you're mad. You didn't even hear the surprise. I got a letter from Barry last week, saying the job finished early, and he'd be on a flight home either today or tomorrow. But I just phoned the airport, and they told me there's another storm coming this way, and all the flights are delayed. So he won't be here tonight. And nobody even cares."

I pushed past Moo. "Quit blubbering," I said. "Just quit it."

She stared at me.

"Go and eat your own meat loaf," I said, my voice dropping even lower, and then I pulled down my steps and climbed up to my room.

I was shaking when I sat down on the floor in front of the window. Taking deep breaths, I looked out into the darkening evening. But the branches of the lone tree in the yard next door had been allowed to grow wild, out of control, and formed a canopy over our whole backyard. The branches not only blocked my view, but also shut out whatever light might find its way into my room through the small window.

March was definitely coming in like a lion. Another snowfall, although I could see that it was more sleet, really — a combination of snow and freezing rain. The storm delaying all flights was keeping me safe for another night. The branches of the tree were coated and glistening.

I don't know what the tree looks like all dressed in green; I haven't been here in summer, and I probably won't ever be. I can imagine that it's pretty, but like I said, right now all it does is block the view. From my window, I can't see anything but the dark and heavy branches.

CHAPTER ELEVEN

❦

The sleet kept up all night, but by morning the sun came out, giving the whole world a false sense of beauty. Well, the beauty wasn't false; the delicate, shimmering ice on the branches and telephone lines and electrical wires made me suck in my breath when I stepped out on to the sidewalk in front of our house. But the ice was causing a lot of trouble. It was almost impossible to get around safely. The roads and sidewalks were sheer glass. Cars and trucks and buses crawled along, but even so, every once in a while, a car would start sliding in a slow, graceful, sideways motion. If it connected with another vehicle, there would be a dull crash. I saw three accidents on the way to school, but they didn't seem to be serious; nothing was moving fast enough for anyone to be badly hurt, and they were just fender benders and dents.

I had to detour around a whole block that was closed off by police cars and repair trucks because a high power cable had broken and fallen under the weight of its coat of ice, so I was late for school. But so were a lot of people. A few teachers didn't even show up until second period. The school had an uncontrolled, holiday feel, although it couldn't break through my own thick layer of icy dread.

During the whole day of classes, all I could think about was last night: Pearl's rigid back, and that steady beat in her neck as I screeched at her. What I'd said, and what I hadn't said. That, and the fact that the skies were clear. The planes would be landing again.

❦

"You're late," Vince said, looking up from the counter, where he was poking white carnations into a piece of foamy green oasis. "Again."

"I know. Sorry," I said. "It's hard walking."

"You were late twice last week. Don't be late, okay, Mercy? I don't like it."

One of the times I was late getting to Vince's recently was because I got a message at school for me to come home right after last class; it was an emergency, the message said. I had run all the way home, gasping, my chest on fire, to find Moo with her foot swollen and propped up on pillows.

"I'm not sure what happened," Moo had mumbled. "I think my ankle turned over. Or maybe I bumped into something. It hurts to walk on it, and I need something for the pain. We're all out of everything. Have you got any cash? Run to the drugstore and get me something extra strength; that's a good girl." She had closed her eyes and taken another long drink.

By the time I'd gone to the drugstore and back home and then to work, I was over an hour late. And the second time was last Saturday morning, and I'd forgotten to wind my clock and just slept in.

"I'm sorry, Vince," I said. "It won't happen again."

I couldn't lose this job. It wasn't just the money, but it really was the only thing that I looked forward to. As I walked toward the counter, I saw the small, round head of Vince's mother. As usual, she was sitting on a straight wooden chair behind the counter, off to one side.

"*Buon giorno,* Mama Gio," I called.

She nodded, smiling. She was eating a big tart. There was always something different in the plastic container beside the coffee-maker. As she chewed, I could see her very pink little tongue inside her shrivelled lips. She said something to Vince. He looked at me and shrugged, and answered his mother.

"What did she say?" I asked Vince.

"Nothing. Nothing, Mercy," he said, reaching for the long spool of florist wire.

But his mother said it again, something that sounded the same as the first time. This time she laughed — a croaky little coughing laugh — then popped the rest of the tart into her mouth.

"It's about me, Vince. I can tell. What's she saying about me?" I asked.

Vince put down the wire. "Listen, Mercy. You know when I didn't want to hire you at first? Remember? And it was Mama who told me to. Because you reminded her of a sad little Italian widow, like herself. So today she says, 'Here's my twin'."

I looked down at my long black skirt. My black laced up boots had damp white squiggles all around the sides, from the snow and ice. I pushed up the sleeves of my black sweater.

"You're lucky, Mercy, lucky you look like an Italian widow," Vince said.

I looked back to Mama Gio.

"Very funny," I said to the tiny crone. "You're a real comedienne, Mama Gio."

She opened her mouth again, her pink tongue darting out, and rocked back and forth, laughing silently.

❦

I was halfway through one of the tarts when Vince came in from a delivery, cold air coming off him like a mist. The tarts were filled with a bottom layer of cream cheese, and then a kind of raspberry filling, and the top of the tart was another layer of pastry, spread with white icing.

"Terrible driving," he said. "I hope this ice melts a bit by tomorrow." He rubbed his hands together. "It's cold, too — not wintry cold, but damp cold. Makes me want soup for supper. Hey Mama, how about soup for supper?" He winked at me.

I looked at Mama Gio, still in her chair in the corner. She was asleep, her head to one side and another uneaten tart clutched in her hand. I pictured Vince helping his mother into the high cab, of his truck, then helping her out again, holding her arm so she wouldn't slip as they went into their house. An old son and an even older mother, living together.

"Vince," I said, spraying the rubbery leaves of a jade plant, "how come you never got married?" I turned around to watch Vince in the room behind me, pouring himself a cup of coffee.

"I was married," he said, spooning sugar into his coffee. He started stirring.

"Oh," I said. After a minute of silence, I continued, "My aunt's been married twice. She's divorced, too."

"My wife died." Vince was still stirring his coffee. Then he put down the spoon and took a sip. "She was sick even before we got married. And it was a long time ago." He took another drink, a longer one this time. "There was a baby, but he didn't make it either."

I turned back to the jade, and started spraying again.

"So it's good for both of us, for her and for me," he said, raising his chin in his mother's direction. "She can't live on her own anymore, and I like company." Carrying his coffee, he went over to her, and put his hand on her shoulder. She didn't move. "I got brothers and sisters, but I'm the only one that stayed here. She used to go and visit them when her health was better, but now it's too hard on her to travel. My cousin Theresa, the one who helps me out here sometimes, lives a few doors down from us. She comes into the house and helps with Mama, too."

Vince softly squeezed the old woman's shoulder. "Mama, rise and shine. Time to go home for supper," he said. Then he spoke in Italian. She opened her eyes, and looked up at him.

I tried to imagine Pearl looking at me like that.

As I was putting on my coat, I stood in front of the main window, looking out. There was a movement across the street, and as I stared, I realized there was someone — a man — standing in the dark doorway of a store, his hands in his pockets. I couldn't see his face, but he was tall. That's all, he was tall.

But suddenly there was a tight pressure in my chest, like a hand squeezing, making it hard for me to breathe. I whirled around and ran into the back room, pressing my hands on to the top of the counter, trying to draw in some air.

Vince looked over at me. He was helping Mama Gio get her arm through the sleeve of her coat.

"Could you give me a ride home?" I asked.

Vince watched me.

"I know it's not far," I said. "But I ..." No more words came. I'd never asked him for a ride before, even when the weather was at its worst.

"Sure," he said. "You don't feel so good?"

"Yeah," I said. "I don't feel so good."

Vince dropped me off a few minutes later. "Feel better soon," he said.

I nodded, getting my key out of my pocket and looking at the dark house. No lights shone from anywhere. As Vince's truck drove away, I looked up and down the empty street. I knew that it probably hadn't been him, B, across the street from Vince's. And even if it was, if he'd found out where I was working, he couldn't have made it here before me, even if he ran all the way. Unless he had a car. As if I were making my life come true with my imagination, car lights swung around the corner. They seemed to be moving too slowly, and I was caught, for a second, in their glare. I turned and ran along the gloomy, narrow path between our house and the neighbours, my boots slipping, my key clutched in my hand. On the back landing, I couldn't see the keyhole in the darkness, but kept stabbing my key in the general direction, listening for footsteps behind me. Finally the key slid in, and I pushed the door open and then slammed it closed behind me, bolting it. I leaned my back against it, waiting for my heart to slow, stop its frenzied knocking against my ribs.

I was hit by the smell: cigarette smoke, fried food, old newspapers. It was the complete opposite of the smells at Santa Marie.

"Moo?" I said, but knew that she must be out, maybe at work. The television would be on if she were at home. I turned on the kitchen light and then went down the hall. Moo's door was open, her ,room empty. Pearl's door was shut.

"I'm home," I said, softly, to the closed door. "Pearl?"

I heard something that could have been a hello, or maybe it was just uh-huh or hm-hmmm. I wanted to go in and say I was sorry, go in and see Pearl sitting on her bed, smiling at me, looking at me the way Mama Gio had looked at Vince. I put my hand on the doorknob, but when there was no other noise, I let go, and went back to the kitchen. I made a peanut butter and honey sandwich and took it and a glass of apple juice to my room, even though I didn't feel like eating. I had to study for a geography test the next morning. I had to keep doing ordinary things, eating and going to work and doing my homework and studying. It was easier not to think about the bad things when I was busy, not to let my imagination scare me into a near coma.

Before I even turned on the light, I managed to get the steps pulled back up. It was really hard, and heavy, to pull them from the top. Then I slid my chair over the edge of the trapdoor. It wouldn't stop anyone from pulling down on the rope and opening the door, but at least the noise of the chair moving would wake me up. If I got to sleep.

Then I flipped on my light, and glanced toward the window. I had a moment of dizzy confusion. Everything was different. I turned off the light, to be able to see outside better, and looked again.

The neighbour's immense old tree had cracked under the weight of all the ice coating its branches, and the top of it had fallen across our yard, smashing the rotting picket fence that divided the two yards. The jagged lower half of the tree jutted tragically into the dusk, and now I could see that the inside of it looked hollow, decayed, as if it had been dying.

The world had opened up outside my window.

I felt a pang of sorrow for the death of that old tree, but I also had a flash of something else. With the tree gone, I felt as if I could breath easier, could see. The lane behind our house was visible now, and I could see the windows and back doors of the houses across the lane from us, and how the light from their lit windows threw patches of brightness on the glassy surface of the snow. And I could see other trees now, too, rising up from other yards. There was one imposing old spruce, black against the falling light, and the tops of lots and lots of tall, lacy trees holding up the sky with their bare arms. I could see all the trees that had been hidden from me until today.

CHAPTER TWELVE

❦

My alarm didn't wake me up the next morning. It was the brightness that did. My room was filled with light.

"No," I said, sitting up and grabbing my clock. I couldn't be late this morning; I had that geography test first class. And my geography teacher didn't accept excuses for missing tests; you had to practically have a doctor's note before she'd let you write it another time. I stared at the hands of the clock. Seven twelve. I wasn't late. The alarm wouldn't go off for another three minutes. As I sat on the edge of my mattress, looking at the dust motes floating in the bleached air by the window, I realized that it was because the tree was gone.

When I got downstairs, creeping stealthily, Pearl's door was still closed. Moo's was still open, and I could see the mound that was her body under the covers. I could hear her snoring. She was alone.

By the time I grabbed my jacket, the sun was starting to work on the ice. The sidewalks were covered in crusty slush, and beads of shining water dripped from everything — branches and eaves and street signs and lamp poles.

It was even warmer after school. I didn't have to be at work until five thirty, but the thought of going home wondering if my mother's door would still be shut, wondering if B would be there — was almost overwhelming. Instead, I walked home with Andrea. From her place it was only another ten minutes to Santa Marie. She looked shocked when I asked her if I could come over for an hour, then nodded her head vigorously.

"Of course," she said, "sure."

When we got to her place, we took a couple of apples from the bowl on the kitchen table and went to her room. I lay down across Andrea's bed. She had a wonderful room. Everything seemed to go together just right. Even her bedspread and curtains were the same material — white with burgundy musical notes all over them — probably because Andrea took piano lessons. She had pretty little collections of things: elephants, and tiny boxes, and seashells.

The rest of Andrea's house wasn't as beautiful as her room. But everything in this room was new — all the furniture and the bedspread and curtains and rug — bought for Andrea by her father when he moved out.

"My mom says this bedroom is a guilt gift," she told me, the first time I saw it. "But I don't care. I still love it."

The first few times I went to Andrea's house, I compared everything in it to mine. Then I had to stop because I started feeling mad at Andrea about it. And then I let the anger transfer to Pearl, and to Moo, the dark green taste of it burning at the back of my throat. But even worse than comparing our houses was comparing our mothers.

It's not like Andrea's mom was perfect. She was pretty nosy, and I've heard her bug Andrea about homework and practising the piano, and she's always brushing Andrea's hair away from her face and saying she looks better without bangs. Each time I was there, she'd barge right in to Andrea's room, showing us something she'd bought, or telling us about a house she'd closed a deal on that day — she's a real estate agent — or asking us to taste something she was making for supper.

Today she tried to give me a bright red sweater.

"This shrunk in the laundry," she said, coming in and waving it over her head like a flag. "It doesn't fit me at all. And Andy can't wear red; it makes her look sallow. But I can tell it would fit you perfectly, Mercy, and with your creamy skin ... well, it would be marvellous. Try it on."

I sat up and put my legs over the edge of the bed.

"Mom," Andrea said.

"Come on, Mercy. It will change you entirely."

"*Mom,*" Andrea said again. "Maybe she doesn't want to change. She looks good like that." She gave a short laugh, as if it were all a joke.

"Nobody likes to wear the same colour all the time, Andrea. I mean, black is very dramatic, but if you throw in a bright colour, it changes the whole look." She held the red sweater up under my chin.

"Look at that. Come here, to the mirror. See how the red reflects upward, giving your skin a pink glow?"

"It's okay, Mrs Leclaire. Thanks, but I couldn't." As Mrs Leclaire had swung the sweater toward me, I saw one of those little pieces of plastic that holds the price tag still attached at the back of the neck. "I think I'm allergic to that kind of wool."

Mrs Leclaire stepped back, still holding the sweater. Her mouth opened, then closed again. "Are you sure, Mercy? You can take it home and try it."

I shook my head. "Thanks anyway," I said.

When she left, Andrea said, "Sorry about that. Just ignore her. That's what I do. She always tries too hard. Sometimes I tell her that's probably why my dad left." She went to the mirror and turned her back to it and looked over her shoulder at herself.

"You say that to her? That's why your dad left?" Andrea's mom bugged her because she tried too hard, and mine didn't try hard enough. You always want what you don't have.

"Sure. She just tells me I don't know what I'm talking about. She's probably right, but I like getting her mad sometimes. It makes me feel better. And she knows I don't mean it. So do you want to go somewhere tomorrow night?" she asked me. "You already said you're not working. We could take a bus over to Portage Place Mall. Or see what movies are playing. Do you think these jeans make my butt look big?"

"No. And I guess we could do something," I said, tracing one of the notes with two little tails over and over with my finger.

"What are you thinking about? You're really quiet." Andrea left the mirror and stood in front of me.

I looked up from the bedspread. "Nothing."

She sat down beside me. "I'll tell you a secret if you'll tell me one."

I made a face. "I don't like that kind of stuff. Like TRUTH OR DARE. It's stupid. Babyish."

Andrea sat up straighter, a hurt look on her face. "I didn't mean it like *that.* I just meant ... I don't know. I just feel like telling you something, but I didn't know how to say it."

"Just say it."

"You won't think I'm dumb or anything?"

"No. Why would I?"

"Because it's a dumb secret. It's about my mom and dad." She bit at the cuticle on her thumb. "You won't tell Kiera or any of them, will you?"

"Andrea, I barely speak to them. Why would I say anything to them about what you tell me?" I shook my head. This girl could just go on and on.

"Okay. This is it. I've been doing the Ouija board every night. Every night I ask it the same question: Will my mother and father get back together? And Merce, it's really freaky, but no matter how many times I ask, it says yes. I think it's going to come true. I've been wishing on everything you can wish on — stars and wishbones and lucky pennies — everything. Come on, don't laugh, Mercy."

"I'm not laughing. But I don't think a Ouija board is a good idea. I don't like them."

"I know. It's just that I keep seeing signs. Everywhere. Like I say, 'If the next car that passes me is white, like my dad's, then he's coming back to us.' And the next car *is* white."

I just nodded.

"See? You think I'm dumb. I can tell. But it's been going on for over two months. Since just after Christmas. I wanted to tell someone, but I thought

Kiera, or Elsbeth, or especially Miki, would laugh at me. They're sick of me talking about my dad; they think I should just let it go, shut up about him. But I wanted to tell someone this so it would seem that it really is possible."

I looked at her delicate face, her skimpy fringe, the begging, intelligent look in her eyes. Her eyes were like the ones you see on those big quiet dogs, the kind of dogs that pull little kids out from under the waves, or old people out of burning buildings.

"Couldn't you tell me even one secret, Mercy? Since I told you mine."

It was hard to tell people things that were important when you weren't used to doing it. And, like Andrea, I had the feeling that once you said the words out loud the dream, or in my case, the nightmare, might become real.

But I opened my mouth anyway. *There's this guy. My aunt's boyfriend, I wanted to say. I'm scared of him, but I can't tell, because it will cause more trouble. Like maybe no one will believe me, and my aunt will hate me because she'll think I'm trying to break them up; and my mother will hate me because there goes our only reliable source of income. And there's also something very wrong with her ... with my mother. I've been getting signs, too, Andrea, but not like yours.*

"Go on."

I could tell she was holding her breath. "Okay," I said. "It's this." Everything in me was screaming to say it, tell her about B. I licked my lips, and then said, "It's my mother." I hadn't meant to say that. That isn't what I meant to tell her.

Andrea nodded. She'd never seen my mother. Never seen Moo. Never been to my house. And I'd never said anything about them. "What?" she finally asked. "What about your mother?"

"She's sort of sick, I guess."

Andrea nodded again. More silence. She had never gone so long without talking.

I thought about Pearl. About how she hardly spoke anymore. How she wouldn't eat. How she wouldn't go out of the house, and just moved from her bed to a chair and back to her bed. *What could I say about it?*

"That's it," I said.

"Okay." There was more silence. It was Andrea's turn to start on the bedspread notes. I watched as she traced a treble clef beside her knee.

"Will she be better soon?"

"I don't know."

"Mercy."

I looked up.

"Is it something, you know, serious? Like, I don't know." Her voice got quieter. "Something bad? Cancer? You don't have to tell me if you don't want to," she said, really quickly, "but it's not like the flu or something, is it?"

I got up and went over to Andrea's books. With my back to her, I ran my finger over their smooth spines. I stopped on *Brave New World.*

"Well, it's definitely not the flu," I said, still not turning around. "It's not really physical, I guess." I pulled the book out of the shelf, and sat down at the desk. Saying it out loud made me see it more clearly. It was physical in that she wasn't sleeping or eating, but what made her stop doing those normal human things? If it wasn't physical, it must be mental.

"Did you like this?" I asked, holding the book, but looking at the pictures of Andrea sitting on her dad's knee, and him wearing a Santa hat; of Andrea and her mother in bathing suits at a beach; of Andrea sitting at the piano and smiling at the camera; of Andrea and her older sister on a snowy hill with their arms around each other's necks.

"No. Did you?"

I studied the pictures of Andrea and her family. "Yeah. I did."

"It was just too bizarre for me. All those metaphors and symbolic meanings. I like it when stuff is straightforward, when you can understand it without all these layers of things underneath that you need to be a genius to figure out. What did you like about it?"

"Nothing in particular. And I should be going. It's almost five thirty."

"I hope your mother gets better soon," Andrea said. "You can talk to me about her anytime you want. That's what friends do, Mercy."

"Don't tell anyone else, okay?" I said.

"I wouldn't. Just like you won't tell the secret I told you."

I looked at Andrea and realized it was true. It was a new feeling. I'd never held anyone else's secrets, only my own.

❦

There were lots of things I liked about *Brave New World,* but I kept thinking about the part where everyone took soma. It was a kind of "happiness" drug that fixed up every ache and pain. It created a chemical haze so you couldn't feel any discomfort or experience any hurt. When I first read about it, I thought it would be great. But as I kept reading, I found out that it also took away the ability to feel any good stuff, too, like really caring about anything or anybody.

Anytime things seem too great, there's got to be a catch.

CHAPTER THIRTEEN

❦

It seemed to be even warmer as I walked to work from Andrea's. I didn't do up my coat, and wasn't hurrying, watching how the sun bounced off puddles and reflected in the store windows. Watching the reflections, I even forgot to watch for B for a few minutes.

"Come on, Mercy, hurry!" Vince had his jacket on and was standing outside the store, looking down the street as if he'd been waiting for me.

"What's up?"

His face had a strange look on it, one I'd never seen before. "Get in the truck."

"Should I put my stuff in the store first?" I saw him locking the door, but he hadn't turned the sign over in the window. It said OPEN FOR BUSINESS. "What is it, Vince?" I didn't like the feeling I was picking up.

"I'll tell you in the truck. Just get in."

I thought something must have happened to his mother. Although why would I be in his truck if there was something wrong with his mother? He would leave me to run the store if he had to go to her.

"It's like this," he said, glancing in his side mirror and then pulling into the street. "Your auntie phoned me about an hour ago, from the hospital, looking for you. She had to call an ambulance this afternoon. For your mother."

I was staring at Vince's profile. "What happened?"

"I'm not so sure. Your auntie, she was pretty upset. She said some things, but they didn't make too much sense. She said to tell you to come to the Emergency at the Health Sciences Centre as soon as you could." I felt him look at me, but now I was staring straight ahead, through the windscreen. The wipers came on every few seconds to clear away the muddy spray thrown up by other cars' wheels.

"You pray, okay, Mercy? You say a prayer for your mama."

Vince let me off in front of the Emergency doors. "I'll park and then come in," I heard him say, but I was already out and running, in through the double doors and up to the wide, semi-circular chest-high counter at one end of the room. Everything seemed too bright, too clear. It was like my brain was snapping pictures, with the flash on, of every little detail.

"Pearl Donnelly," I said to a nurse sitting there. She looked up. She had hard lines etched around her mouth. More deep furrows radiated from the corners of her eyes and across her forehead.

"I'm looking for Pearl Donnelly. She's my mother."

The nurse glanced at something on her desk. "Come this way," she said. I followed her along a hall where curtains divided areas. There were voices, and somewhere a baby was crying. We got to another hall with at least a dozen doors. The nurse wore a faded green cardigan over her white top. The sleeves of the sweater were too long. Her white trousers were too short, and her ankles were thick. She stopped outside a doorway, read the chart held on the door by a piece of hard plastic, then looked at me. "She's in here," she said. Her eyes were the same green as her sweater, and they looked sad, somehow. Or maybe just tired. They didn't fit her either. "Are you alright?"

I don't know why she asked me that. And I didn't know if I was alright or not. I didn't feel anything, like I was pumped full of soma, but I knew I needed to nod at her, and when I did, she opened the door a bit and put her head in.

"Her daughter is here," she said, and took her head out and stepped away from the door. "They'll be moving her upstairs in a little while," she said, then left.

Without warning, the soma disappeared, and my legs filled with water. I knew I couldn't walk into the room. I couldn't move, or I would fall. There was the sound of chair legs scraping against a hard floor, and a swishing noise, and then Moo appeared in the doorway. Her face was like a huge, white moon: her features only shallow impressions on the blank surface. She grabbed my wrist.

"She'll be okay, Mercy," she said. "They pumped her stomach."

"What happened?" My voice came out a monster croak.

Moo's eyes shifted to my hair, my shoulder, beyond me, out to the hall. "She took pills. The painkillers, those extra strength you got me. She took too many."

I waited for her eyes to come back. Eventually they did, her pupils lighting on mine for the briefest of moments, then floating away again. I didn't ask the question, but Moo answered it.

"I don't know what happened, Mercy. If she just got mixed up, and didn't know she took so many, or what. She's been getting lots of headaches, you know, and she asked me for something, for the pain. I gave her the bottle. I didn't think anything — she had headaches — I never thought ... and it was too quiet in her room for too long. I should have realized something was wrong." The impressions that were her eyes and nose and mouth moved in and out of focus, as if translucent clouds were passing in front of them.

The water drained away from my legs, out through the ends of my toes, and I took a step, and then another. I pulled my wrist free from Moo's grasp and went to the side of the bed.

"She'll be alright, the doctor said." Moo's voice was faint, as faraway as her face had been. "But they're going to keep her here for a few days, at least. They have to; it's procedure, he told me, when ... in these cases. Mercy?"

The monitor beeped quietly beside Pearl. Her eyes were closed, and she was so still, her breathing so light and shallow that I had to lean down close, to make sure that she really was breathing. Then I moved a step back and studied her face, the thin delicate lines of her cheekbones, and the hollows under them. Her eyelids and lips were smooth; lying on her back like this, there were no wrinkles anywhere on her face. I hadn't seen her lying on her back for a long time; lately it seemed she always slept on her side, all curled into herself, her back to the door.

This way she looked young, and like someone else. She looked like she must have looked when she was my age.

"I hate you," I said. My voice came out loud, too loud in the white, quiet room; the croaking monster grown brave. "I hate you for this," I said, even louder than the first time, so loud that I realized it was a shout, but it wasn't me shouting — it was the monster with the camera eyes. "Do you hear me? I hate you!"

I turned and ran, past Moo, out of the room and down the hall toward the high desk, where I almost bumped into Vince, and out into the bright late-afternoon sunlight. I ran and ran, down sidewalks, across streets, dodging traffic and people, running, running, until I couldn't run anymore — running away from the fact that it was my fault my mother had almost died.

CHAPTER FOURTEEN

❦

I didn't go to see Pearl the next day, or the day after that. She was alright physically, Moo told me, but they thought they should keep her there, at the hospital. She was in the psychiatric ward, Moo said, for observation.

The psychiatric ward. That was for people who were called names like schizophrenics, and delusional, and psychopathic. And those were the good names. What about crazy, nuts, lunatic? None of them were names for my mother; they were names for other people. I shouldn't have been surprised. I had realized, when I said it out loud to Andrea, that my mother's problem wasn't a physical one. It was a mental one.

I couldn't go to work, either. I left a message on the answering machine at the store, calling after hours on purpose, telling Vince I wouldn't be in for a few days. He'd probably fire me, but I just couldn't look at his face, thinking about what he knew, how he had looked as I'd run by him. That strange expression that might have been pity, but also might have been disgust. I wouldn't blame him if he was disgusted, or if he fired me.

I did go to school, because no one there knew anything was different. Andrea asked me a few times if everything was alright, and finally I told her my mom got really sick and had to go to the hospital. She said okay really quickly, and reached out and put her hand on my arm. I couldn't — look at her when she did that, but I didn't move my arm away.

I didn't want to see Pearl. I had to put some space between us for a little while, otherwise, when I looked at her, the top of my head might burst open, and the monster would fully emerge. Plus I was scared of what I would see if I went to the hospital, to the place she was staying.

I'd seen old movies like *The Snake Pit* and *One Flew Over the Cuckoo's Nest* on late-night television, those horrible images of padded walls and screaming, rolling-eyed patients in straitjackets. I knew it probably wasn't really like that, at least not anymore, but I was afraid of what I might see. Of how I might find Pearl.

I was hanging in a kind of limbo, waiting. Waiting to find out if my mother would ever come home. Waiting for B. Where was he? Moo hadn't said anything more about him. I didn't want to ask; maybe if I did she'd say, "He'll be here in an hour," or something unbearable like that. I started thinking that maybe something else had happened; that maybe he had phoned and said he wasn't coming, after all. I realized longer and longer periods of time were going by without me thinking about him; I was thinking about Pearl. But still, I pulled up my steps and slid the chair over my door every night.

"Aren't you planning to go to the hospital?" Moo

asked me, on the third day. It was after school, and I was dumping a box of macaroni into a pot of boiling water on the stove. I turned to face her.

"How long will she be there?"

Moo chewed an ice cube. It made hard, painful sounds between her teeth. "They finished the psychiatric evaluation yesterday. Now she's on medication, and I think she has to go to classes or something."

"Classes?"

"No. Not classes. I mean therapy. Talking to different people — psychiatrists, or psychologists, about mental illness. Depression."

I couldn't see Pearl talking to strangers. She wouldn't even talk to me. I took a wooden spoon from the drawer and stirred the macaroni. The small curved pieces of pasta were spinning and frothing in the boiling water. It reminded me of what my brain must look like about now.

"For how long?" I asked again. *Mental illness.*

"She didn't know. She won't say much." Moo started crying. "Do you want to know something? It's all my fault. My fault," she repeated, "and I'm quitting. I'm never telling anybody anything again. No more futures. Nothing."

"What do you mean?" I asked, my voice snappish.

Moo got up and tore a square of paper towel off the roll lying on the counter. She wiped her eyes and then crumpled the towel into one fist.

"It was that last reading," she said. "I told you she wouldn't let me do a reading after the one a few weeks ago."

"The tarot cards?"

"It wasn't them," she said. "That part was okay.

But then I looked at her palm. And what I saw there, something I'd never noticed before ..." She wiped her eyes again. "I don't know why I didn't keep my big mouth shut. Why did I tell her? If I hadn't, she'd be home with us now."

"What did you say?"

"I saw the St Andrew's Cross," she explained. "Right here, on her Mount of Venus." Moo touched the fleshy mound of skin near her thumb. "I'd never noticed it before, but suddenly there it was, and I told her what it means." She shook her head, her lips tightening.

The macaroni was turning mushy.

"It means that you will find a happy love only once in your life. A one and only love. And since Pearl was happy, so in love with your father, I was basically telling her she'd never be happy again, never love again. And that's what did it. Pushed her too far."

I turned off the stove. "Moo." I closed my eyes for a minute. "That's not why it happened."

"Yes, it is. But I don't want to talk about it anymore."

"That's not why," I repeated. I knew the real reason. It was what I had done, said, screamed at her. It was me who had pushed her too far. "Has she said anything else? About me?"

The pot was hardly bubbling now, the murky water just giving a burp now and then.

"I told her you felt awful about everything, and that she should call you."

The spoon hit the counter as if it were held by some other hand. "How do you know how I feel? I never said I felt awful. You never asked." I was yelling. Again. I smacked the counter a second time, and this time the spoon cracked in two, the wet end flying into the air and hitting the fridge door, and then dropping to the floor. I looked at the broken handle I was still holding. "You don't know a thing. About me, or about anything," I said, quietly this time, throwing the handle into the sink, and going upstairs.

That evening I went to the library. On the computer there, under MAIN SUBJECTS, I slowly typed in mental illness.

It seemed even harder to type the words than it had been to say them out loud, to Andrea. Typing them, seeing them on the screen in front of me, made them even more real, in a strange way.

There were long lists of books, with names like *Lost in Darkness: A Memoir of Madness,* but I didn't want to think about the word "madness," because that reminded me of the woman in the novel *Jane Eyre.* Bertha, Mr Rochester's poor wife, was called a lunatic, who needed to be locked in a cell.

I ran through more titles with medical names — neurosis, psychosis, paranoia — and then stopped at one. *Helping When Your Loved One Is Depressed,* it said. It wasn't threatening. Helping means you can do something about it. Your loved one. I did love her, no matter what I had said to her, or how I had treated her. Depressed. Depressed. It was a simple word. I heard people moaning about being depressed all the time, tossing it around casually. Kids at school: "I'm so depressed. I have to study all weekend. I have a detention. I can't get the car this weekend." People on the bus, or at Santa Marie: "I'm so depressed. Our team lost the hockey tournament. Another winter coming on. My mother-in-law is coming to stay for a whole week."

All trivia. Homework, weather, petty annoyances.

I went to the shelves and found the book, sat down at one of the long tables, and opened the first page. There was a checklist, to determine whether your "loved one" really is depressed. I skimmed the twenty-five questions. At the bottom it said that if you answered yes to any six of the above items, then chances are your loved one is suffering from depression.

I had answered yes to twenty of the twenty-five questions .

In part two, the book said, we'll address what you can do if this is the case.

I read a bit further, then went and gathered some other books from the shelves. I put the book on depression into the middle of the pile, and then checked them all out.

I walked home, the books cradled against my chest.

My mother wasn't crazy. She didn't have the blues, and she wasn't a bit down. She was depressed. She'd probably been depressed for a long time, maybe starting before she lost her job, maybe before she gave up on her Donnelly's Desserts dream, maybe before her unemployment money ran out and she stopped looking for another job. Maybe before she refused to go down to the welfare office, maybe even before B had come into our lives. And she'd grown steadily worse and worse, and we hadn't said, or done, anything about it.

No. That's not completely true.

Moo had started drinking more, and I'd fallen in love with black.

CHAPTER FIFTEEN

❦

This time I walked through the doors at the main entrance of the hospital. At the information counter, I said "Pearl Donnelly." The woman punched the computer keys and then said, in a bored voice, without looking up, "A6. Room 620."

I stood there another minute, thinking she might tell me that I'd missed visiting hours, or that I wasn't allowed to go to that ward without some kind of appointment, or even crazier, that she'd have to check my pockets for sharp items.

But when she kept typing on the computer as if I wasn't there, I went to the elevator. My backpack was heavy and bulky; I'd come right from school.

When I got out at the sixth floor, I somehow expected to be met by a padlocked door, or at least a kind of wire barrier. But this looked like any other hospital corridor. There was a counter where a bunch of silver, decorated helium balloons swayed, floating on long ribbons that were tied to a handle of a desk drawer. A man in a white short-sleeved top stood behind the counter. The bar on the left side of his top said J. POPOV, R.N.

"Yes?" He smiled at me.

"Pearl Donnelly," I said again. "Can I see her?" I cleared my throat. "She's my mother."

"Sure," he said. "Pearl's in 620. Go down that hall, to your left, and her room's on the right side." As I started to leave, he called after me. "Do you mind leaving your backpack here?"

I stopped and took it off. "Can I give her something?" I unzipped the pouch and took out my gift.

He smiled again. "Cool," he said. "Listen, if she's not in her room, she might be in the rec room. Or in the dining room. They're both at the end of the hall."

I passed people who must have been patients because they weren't wearing jackets or coats or boots. They also weren't wearing pyjamas and robes. They had on regular clothes, jeans and T-shirts, or sweats and trainers. One woman had a Walkman over her head, and was power walking up and down the hall, chewing gum and swinging her elbows to what might be the beat of the music in her ears.

I stopped outside the open wooden door that displayed a large six-two-zero. As I stood there, I heard the slow swoosh of paper against paper; a page turning. I went in.

There was a bed, and a curtain dividing the room. A woman with dark, tightly curled hair was sitting on top of the neatly made bed. Her legs were crossed, tailor style, and she wore navy sweatpants and a baggy white T-shirt with a black-and-white spotted cow on it. DRINK MILK was written in letters coming from the cow's mouth.

The woman was writing in a notebook in her lap, and looked up as I came in.

"Hi," she said.

"Hi," I tried to say, but again, I had to clear my throat.

"You Mercy?"

I nodded.

The woman tipped her head toward the curtain. "Your mom's in the next bed."

I hesitated at the thin white curtain. "Pearl?" I called.

"Yeah. Here." Her voice came to me clearly, and I realized that the curtain wasn't all the way around, but just pulled between the two beds. I went to the foot of her bed and stood there. Pearl was propping herself up against her pillow. She rubbed her eyes with her fists.

"I guess I dozed off," she said.

I looked out the window beside her bed. Straight below was a parking lot filled with cars. Across were other buildings, and in the spaces between buildings were the tops of bare trees. Everything — the roofs of the cars in the lot, the buildings, the distant trees — had the same colourless, dusty, tired-of-winter look. On the ledge outside the window was a pigeon. It was looking in at us, neck shimmering, iridescent green. I put my hand up to the side of my head, touching my hair, this hair, and remembering the pigeon in Peanut Park.

"I call him Frank," Pearl said.

"Why?"

"He looks like a Frank."

"Maybe it's a girl," I said.

"Maybe. You can sit down if you want." There was a straight chair against the heater under the window. The only other furniture was a little bedside table with three drawers.

I sat down.

"You'll get too hot. It's warm in here. You should take off your coat."

"No. I'm okay like this." So far we hadn't looked at each other's face. I decided to go first. Pearl seemed to be more interested in Frank than she was in me right now.

She didn't look any different than she had when I'd seen her last. Maybe thinner, if that was possible. She was wearing a pair of brown corduroy trousers and her green sweatshirt. Moo must have brought them from home. I thought there would have been some subtle change.

"This place isn't like I thought," I said. I turned sideways in the chair so that I could watch Frank, too. He gave a peck on the window, a tiny chink like tapped china, then dropped his head to give another half-hearted peck at the concrete ledge beneath him. He turned his head and looked into the air, as if he were judging the distance between the concrete beneath his feet and one of the trees so far away. From the side, the one eye visible to me was a dark, shining jewel in a bed of soft grey velvet. He looked toward the glass again, lifting his feet, his neck pumping and fidgety.

"He'll fly away now. That's how he moves every time he's going to take off."

She was right. The pigeon shifted its body in a slow, waddling step, unfolded its wings, and, with one flap, pushed away from the ledge.

"He'll be back," Pearl said.

I turned around in my chair. Now that Frank had left, there didn't seem to be anything to talk about. "I brought you something," I said, and held out the mask. "I made it in art class." We were supposed to leave them; the drama students needed them this week, but I took mine. I hadn't bothered to tell Mr Lindstrom.

"It's a sunflower," Pearl said. "So bright."

I put the mask up to my face, holding it by the chin. Looking at Pearl through the eyeholes gave me the same sensation as my own tunnel vision trick.

"I'm glad you came, Mercy. I hoped you would." Pearl did something that I think was supposed to be a smile. It was an uncoordinated and tight movement at the corners of her lips that reminded me of the way I had to pull the papier mâché off the balloon form I had used — slowly, slowly, not too fast, or the whole thing might start to crack. Pearl's would-be smile ended before anything cracked, or came undone.

I watched her, just her face, with the dull washed-out green wall a backdrop. And she kept staring at the mask. Something was happening to my own face inside the pasty smell of the hardened papier mâché. It was as if a blowtorch was at work on the shadowed, secret backs of my eyeballs. After a few seconds, the blowtorch moved down behind my nose, to the back of my throat, dragging at the corners of my lips as it went.

I won't cry, I won't cry, I told myself.

"Did you do it on purpose?" I whispered, asking the question that had been hammering inside my skull for four days. "Did you mean to take all those pills?"

Pearl's face was as still as the mask. "I don't know."

"You can't cop out like that, Pearl. You can't say you don't know. You have to tell me. I need to know." *If it was my fault,* I added, inside.

"Everything is so mixed up in my head," Pearl said.

"How could you do that to *me?*" I asked, choking on the tears that were somehow coming up my throat, and into my mouth, instead of from my eyes.

"I didn't do it to you, Mercy. I wasn't thinking of hurting you. It wasn't about you. Or anyone. It wasn't anyone's fault. I keep telling Moo that. I just wanted my own hurting to stop. I remember that much — that it hurt too much. My head. Everything."

It wasn't anyone's fault. The same words the book had said. Depression can happen due to some shock, or it can come on for reasons nobody really understands. There isn't always a specific cause.

There was a sudden muffled flurry against the glass behind me, but Pearl's eyes didn't leave the mask. I was having a hard time breathing. The mask was suffocating me, but it was also protecting me. If I took it away, I wouldn't be able to say any more. And she would see me crying.

"But how could you?" I asked, the tears letting the monster emerge more and more. It was growling now. I knew what the library book had said, how you can't blame them, can't ask them for answers. That it's a sickness, not something the person can control through sheer will.

But I couldn't control what the mask was saying, either, just like I couldn't stop crying. "You would leave me alone, with only Moo and ..." I stopped myself from saying B's name. And I didn't know whether I meant leaving me alone right now, or forever. "I can't do everything, Pearl. You shouldn't expect me to know how to do everything, alone." Hiccuping sounds were coming out of the thin, lipless mouth of the mask.

"Mercy. Baby. I'm sorry. I'm so, so sorry. I know you must hate me." And Pearl put her face down into her cupped hands. Her shoulders shook.

Mom, I mouthed, against the damp, warm opening of the mask. *Mommy.* I closed my eyes against the wet burning. *I didn't mean it when I said that, that day in Emergency. I don't hate you,* my lips said, no sound coming out of the mask mouth. *I love you. I'm so scared. I don't know what to do, about anything. Couldn't you see what was happening, all those months, with B? Help me.*

"You're so much stronger than I am, Mercy," Pearl said, into her hands.

I couldn't breathe. I pulled the mask away and put it by Pearl's feet. She was still crying. I don't know if I'd seen her cry before. Ever. She hasn't seen me cry since I was about nine years old. I stood and walked away from her.

At the door, I looked back. All I could see, through the thin, gauzy layer of tears that made everything seem as if it were underwater, was the end of Pearl's roommate's bed, the white curtain, and Frank, his shining head tilted to one side, watching me leave.

CHAPTER SIXTEEN

❦

I woke up on my birthday with a dull ache behind my eyes, and something prickly at the back of my throat each time I swallowed. Sixteen years old, on the 15th of March. The ides of March, according to the ancient Roman calendar.

"Beware the ides of March," the soothsayer in Shakespeare's *Julius Caesar* proclaims. Caesar doesn't listen to the old guy, and he gets stabbed, fatally, in the back. His murderer is his best friend, Brutus. It's hard for Caesar to believe, because everyone else has betrayed him, and he never suspected his best friend would, too. *Et tu?* he says to his friend, "You too?"

Just as I was leaving for school the phone rang.

"Mercy?"

"Oh. Hi, Vince." I didn't know if he could hear the embarrassment in my voice. I knew I'd let him down by not going to work since that day he took me to the hospital. It had nothing to do with him, but I kept thinking that when I saw him, that horrible, unreal, soma sensation I'd felt in the Emergency room would come back to me. Now he was probably phoning to tell me I was fired. A perfect birthday surprise.

Pearl had been in the hospital for over a week, but I hadn't gone back since that one time. Moo goes to see her every day, and reports to me what's happening. I don't ask, and don't say anything, but she keeps following me around the house, telling me what group session Pearl went to that day, and what individual counselling she was getting. That her medication was a kind of antidepressant that would take a few weeks to really kick in, the doctor told Moo. It would regulate the imbalances in certain brain chemicals, increase her appetite, help her sleep. In the meantime they were giving her something mild, temporary, so she could get some rest.

"None of the medication they're giving her is addictive though," Moo said, trailing after me as I went into the hall. "The doctor said they'll monitor her progress, and as she improves, they might be able to decrease the dosage."

The steps leading to my bedroom were up; Moo has a hard time getting around them to the bathroom when they're down. It's a real tight squeeze for her; I know Moo's up when my steps are up.

"Well, that's a blessing, isn't it, Moo?" I asked, reaching for the rope. "We don't need any more addictions in this family."

Moo's bottom lip started a little dance. "I just thought you would want to know what's happening with your mother. She told me to tell you that you could come to a counselling session at the hospital. One of the therapists said it would be good for you. For you both. And she said to tell you things should be better soon. For you."

I felt the hairy thickness of the rope. "What does that mean?"

"I don't know," Moo said. "She just said that. Tell

Mercy things will be better soon. And she asked lots of other stuff about you . If you're alright."

"When haven't I been?" I had said, and then yanked on the rope so hard that Moo had to step away to avoid getting hit as the steps crashed down.

"So listen," Vince told me over the phone, this birthday morning, "I got a bit of a problem on my hands. I talked to your aunt, on the phone — did she tell you? And I told her you didn't have to come back to work until you felt ready, but I just got a call. I need to make a big delivery, and it has to be at four thirty today. Could you come by on your way home? Just for an hour, until I get back. That's all it will take, there and back. Theresa can't make it. It would really help me, Mercy."

I swallowed, feeling my saliva scratch all the way down. He wasn't firing me. "Yeah. I can come," I said, wondering how many bosses would let someone take a week off just because they didn't want to see his face in case it brought back a bad memory. I couldn't say no, no matter how awful I felt. "Sure. I'll be there by four o'clock."

I hung up. *Happy Birthday to me,* I thought. At least I still have a job. My sixteenth birthday, and my mother is in the psychiatric ward at the hospital; my aunt is sleeping off a hangover; I'm coming down with something, and now I have to go to work.

"And don't forget wallowing in self-pity," I said out loud, putting one arm into my jacket. The phone rang again. Probably Vince, telling me I'd have to stay even later.

"Yeah?" I said, shrugging the other arm in, cradling the phone between my cheek and shoulder.

There was a second of silence.

"Hello. Hello?" I said, frowning, taking the receiver in my hand.

"Mercy? Mercy baby? That you?"

Time stopped.

"Hey, I've missed your sweet voice. Six whole months. You must be really grown-up by now. Have you missed me, too?"

The phone receiver was on fire. It was burning my cheek and my ear and my hand.

"Listen, I'm still here. I was supposed to get back to Canada earlier, but there were some snags, and I couldn't get away when I'd planned to. But now I've got everything straightened out, so I'll be there in a couple of days. You tell Maureen that. I've been phoning, but there's never any answer. Where have you all been? Mercy? Will you tell her? Just a few more days. I can't wait to see all of you again, get back to the way we were."

I dropped the receiver. It fell to the floor with a heavy thud, and lay at my feet like a black, dead thing. But it wasn't completely dead; it could still speak.

"Mercy?" The voice was faraway, even further away than the other side of the world, a tiny cartoon voice travelling out of the circle of holes, calling me, calling me.

I left it on the floor and ran out, forgetting to lock the door.

❦

The day dragged. All I thought about was getting through my classes, then standing behind the counter at Vince's and hoping not too many customers came in, and finally crawling home and into bed. A few days. B had said a few days; I could sleep and sleep, at least tonight. I couldn't swallow without tensing my shoulders.

Before last class I spotted Andrea, talking to Elsbeth and Miki and Kiera by her locker. I hadn't seen her all day. As I walked toward them, Miki glanced in my direction, and said something, and then they all stepped away from one another. It was completely obvious; they'd been talking about me.

"What's up?" I asked, looking at Andrea.

"Nothing," she answered. "Nothing," as if I'd asked her twice. Her cheeks were pink, and her eyes, well, all of the white parts were showing. "So, anyway, Elsbeth, I'll come over right after supper and you can help me with that assignment."

"Okay," Elsbeth said.

Yeah, right. As if Elsbeth could help anyone with any assignment.

"What are you doing tonight?" Elsbeth asked me. I saw Miki touch her elbow against Elsbeth's.

"I have to go to work for a while," I said.

"Oh, do you? That's too bad," Elsbeth said. Kiera and Miki looked down at their binders. Andrea spotted something on the toe of her boot, and bent over to rub at it. When she straightened up, her cheeks were an even darker pink.

"Yeah, isn't it," I said, looking at Andrea's cheeks.

We stood there until Miki said, "Well, I guess we should be going.

"Yeah," Andrea and Elsbeth and Kiera said, together.

"See you, Mercy," Andrea called over her shoulder, and they walked away. I walked in the other direction, but turned and saw that they had stopped and were talking again, halfway down the hall.

I could imagine what they were talking about, although I really couldn't believe Andrea would do that to me. I'd told her my mother had to go into the hospital. I'd told her my mother had some kind of problem that wasn't physical. So she probably put two and two together, and now was spreading around the secret.

Let her. *Go ahead, Andrea,* I thought. *Tell whatever you want about me.*

And she didn't even say, "Happy Birthday." We talked about our birthdays a long time ago, but Andrea's is exactly one month past mine, April 15th. So you'd think she would have remembered. *I don't care what you say about my mother, or that you forgot my birthday, Andrea,* I thought. *I've got more important things to worry about.*

I don't know why I had been afraid to face Vince. When I saw him, looking at me anxiously from under his old blue baseball cap, all I felt was a nudge of fire behind my eyes, but I blinked hard, and it passed.

"How're you doing?" he asked, quietly.

I managed a smile. "I'm okay. Hey, thanks for giving me some time off."

"No problem. I'll be gone maybe an hour, hour and

a half, at the most. Mama will look after you, right, Mama?" He spoke to her in Italian, and the old lady waved her hand up at him, shooing him away like a pesky fly.

"You can fill up the containers from the cooler, if you're bored," he told me. "Put some new wrapping paper on the roll. And just do a general tidy-up. The place gets messy without you around to keep things in order."

I did what he asked. Mama Gio drank coffee and crunched at a hard *biscotto* from the container. There were only three customers, each just picking up a plant or a quick bouquet on their way home from work.

I stood behind the counter, looking out at the cars going by on the street. Glancing behind me, I saw Mama Gio had dozed off.

"So here we are, eh, Mama Gio?" I said, just to hear my own voice in the quiet store. She didn't stir. "Here we are, the two women in black. Want to hear my sad story?" Her chin rested on her flat chest.

I turned back to the windows at the front of the store, half smiling, even though nothing was funny. "I can't talk to anyone except an old lady who's asleep, who wouldn't understand me even if she weren't." I took a damp cloth from under the counter and slowly wiped off the bits of fern and particles of dirt that clung to the surface.

"So," I said. "This is my screwed-up life. I'm trying really hard to hold it all together, and sometimes I think I'm almost making it. I'm not a loser, no matter what certain people might think. I've got this job, and I've got a friend — a so-called friend, right now — for the first time in my life. And I'm doing okay in school." I kept wiping in big, swirling circles, watching the damp patterns the cloth made.

"But my mother is in the psychiatric ward at the hospital. I don't know when she's coming home, and when she does, what she's going to be like. And then there's B: my aunt's boyfriend. I can't even say his name out loud. That's how much he scares me. And he's coming home, too." I slapped the counter lightly with the rag. "Now what, Mama Gio? Now what?"

"I light a candle for you," said a crackly little voice behind me.

I whirled around. "What?"

"Tonight, when my Vince take me to church, I light a candle. I pray for you. And for your mama, and for your auntie. Maybe I light lotsa candles. To give you more strength. Power."

I stared at her. Her little brown eyes weren't crinkled up in their usual smile. The rosary beads started clinking through her fingers.

"But ... but ... you don't speak English."

"Who say?"

"Vince — he always talks to you in Italian. You only speak Italian back. I just thought ..." My mind was racing over all the things I'd just said. About my mother. About B.

"You never ask me. You never talk to me," Mama Gio said. Her English voice was the same as her Italian — high and quick.

"But you and Vince ..." was all I could say.

"Listen," Mama Gio said. "Could be someday you go Italy with your mama. To live. Long, long time pass. You learn Italian, maybe not so good, but you learn. But with your mama, you always speak English, no?"

I watched her little mouth, the words pouring out.

"You no speak Italian with your mama. Why you speak to her with words you have to look for? Words you don't find? With the people in your heart, you speak with words from your heart. So is like for me and my son. *Capisci?*"

I looked at the floor between us.

"Come. Come down, to me."

I crouched in front of her. She reached out and patted my cheek. Her fingers were gnarled, the skin papery and dry, like they were dusted with fine powder. "I light candles. I say prayers. Maybe you get some help. But lots is up to you."

"I know," I said.

The door slammed. "Where is everybody?" Vince called.

I stood up. "Here."

"Thanks for helping me out. You call me when you want to come back to work steady again."

"You know what Vince? I'll be in tomorrow. If you can use me, that is."

"You sure?"

"Yeah. I'll be here tomorrow. Saturday morning, ten o'clock."

"Okay." He glanced at his mother, then back to me. "Mama been keeping you company?"

"*Sì,*" Mama Gio said, and looked at me. One eye closed a little. It might have been a wink, but I wasn't sure.

As I walked home, I thought about Mama Gio

lighting candles for me. And I held on to my anger at Andrea, letting it fill me up. It was good to feel mad at Andrea, instead of at Pearl. And at Moo. It made me stop thinking about how much my head hurt.

Some friend. *Et tu,* Andrea.

CHAPTER SEVENTEEN

❦

I dropped my stuff by the back door. All I wanted was my bed. And this day to be over.

There was a muffled sound from the living room. I stopped, my hand on the back of a chair. "Moo?" I called. Nothing. Then I heard it again. A kind of whisper, or maybe it was just Moo asleep in front of the television again. I looked into the hall. But there were no lights on; no glow from the television. The hand tightened in my chest like it had the night I thought I saw B across from Santa Marie.

"Is that you, Moo?" I called. B had said in a few days. But what if he was here all along? Following me, watching me. Waiting for me.

"Moo!" I yelled. "Answer me."

There was another moment of silence, except for the thrashing of my heart against my ribs. Then, "Yes, Mercy. It's me. Come here."

I went down the hall. "Why are all the lights —" I said, but then a lamp came on with a blink.

"Surprise! Surprise! Happy Birthday!" Moo's voice was loud and cheery. The other voices weren't quite as enthusiastic.

It couldn't be. Please. Let this not be happening. I closed my eyes for a second, the whole sad scene burned on the inside of my eyelids, praying that when I opened them Moo wouldn't be standing in the middle of the room, a pointed cardboard birthday hat perched on her head instead of her turban; and her hair, celebrating its freedom, hanging on her shoulders in thin, crimpy curls. That Andrea wouldn't be standing in one corner, holding one of those little New Year's Eve paper blowers. That Miki and Elsbeth and Kiera wouldn't also be holding party poppers, sitting in a row on the ratty, worn-out plaid couch, like those three see-no, hear-no, tell-no-evil monkeys. That there weren't balloons stuck to the peeling wallpaper and droopy curtains. That there weren't bowls of crisps and gloopy-looking dip and cans of no-name soda on the coffee table stained with white rings.

I opened my eyes. It was all still there. This time I also saw a pile of presents in the big hollow seat of the chair by the window.

"Are you surprised, Mercy?" Moo asked, coming toward me, her arms open wide. She was wearing her dress-up caftan, the black one with tiny yellow suns around the neckline. She slowly swooped toward me, bat-like, and enveloped me in a thick haze of Obsession perfume and Beefeater gin. Her make-up was already smearing, the blue from her eyelids making a squiggly descent to the sides of her eyes, her lipstick a slash of blood. Not so much a bat as a hefty bride of Frankenstein, except for the hat. I saw that the elastic keeping it on was cutting a deep and painful-looking rut into her extra chin.

I stepped back, out of her arms, and stared at her. Even though her eyes had the usual glazed and slightly unfocused look I hated, something else was there, something I wasn't sure about.

"It's a sweet sixteen party, Mercy. Turning sixteen is an event. I couldn't let it go by without doing something special. It was perfect timing," she went on. "The girls just got here a few minutes before you. And Vince was in on it, too. I got him to ask you to work for a bit so everyone could get here."

I glanced at Andrea. I could feel the imagined knife in my spine twist, and glared at her, but she had the guiltless look down perfectly. All she did was let her shoulders slide up and down in a don't-ask-me gesture.

"Now, you girls — have some crisps and pop. I'll get the sandwiches. Mercy, put on some music. Let's get this party started!"

There was silence when Moo left. I was still standing in the doorway.

Finally Miki said, "What CDs have you got, Mercy?" She leaned forward and took a crisp, putting it to her lips and taking a tiny nibble, as if she were testing to make sure it was an acceptable brand.

"I just have tapes. For my Walkman. We only have a —" I stopped before I said "hi-fi." That's what Moo and Pearl called the old stereo cabinet with the turntable and radio. A hi-fi. God. "Moo has this old record collection. Or we could listen to the radio."

"What kind of records?" Elsbeth asked.

"All kinds," I said "Look for yourself."

Elsbeth and Kiera knelt in front of the shelf beside the stereo cabinet. Hundreds of records were lined up. They started pulling some out. "Hey, cool,"

Kiera said. "Jim Morrison. My parents saw his grave when they were in Paris two years ago. Put this on."

I took it and opened the lid of the stereo cabinet, started the turntable, and set the arm on to the record.

"So is that your mom? Moo?" Miki asked, pushing her glasses up the bridge of her nose. Her voice sounded perfectly normal. As if she didn't know.

"No," I answered, staring hard at her. "My aunt."

"Her mom's sick," Andrea said, her glance flickering toward me. "She's still in the hospital, right, Mercy?"

I just narrowed my eyes at her.

"Look at this," Elsbeth said. "Vanilla Fudge."

Miki joined them, pulling out another record. "The Archies? The Archies!" She laughed, and pushed it back in, pulling out the one beside it. "George Harrison."

"Who?" Kiera asked.

"George Harrison."

"Wasn't he the Beatle who got shot?"

"No," Andrea answered. "That was John Lennon."

I pulled at Andrea's sleeve. "Andrea. Come with me, to the bathroom." My voice was a harsh whisper under Jim Morrison's .

I dragged her into the bathroom and shut the door.

"You're supposed to be my friend. I can't believe you. I just can't believe you."

"Why are you blaming me? You aunt phoned me, a few days ago. She said she found my name and number — that you'd written them down by the phone — and she asked if I was your friend. I told her yes, and she started talking about this surprise party. What was I supposed to do?" She stuck out her chin.

I put my fingers on my forehead and leaned against them. "It's not just that."

"What do you mean?"

"Today, in school, you were ..." I stopped. I thought about the way they were whispering and looking at me. "That's what you were talking about when I came up to you? Tonight?"

"Of course. And you know Elsbeth. She messes everything up. We were talking about meeting to walk here together. About your presents, Mercy."

I kept my forehead against my fingers.

"You know, I told your aunt you probably wouldn't like it, but she insisted; told me to invite some kids. I didn't know what to do. What did you think we were talking about?"

I raised my head. "I thought ... maybe, you know. My mom and everything."

Andrea rolled her eyes. "God, Mercy. It's so *hard* being your friend." Her voice was angry, but her face had the same hopeful look as her mother's when she had tried to give me the sweater.

"Don't you get it yet? You can trust me."

Knuckles rapped on the door. "Sammies for everyone!" Moo called. "Come out, girls."

Andrea and I trooped out of the bathroom.

Moo was standing in the middle of the living room, holding the plate of sandwiches in front of her. "Here we are, everyone, gather around," her voice sang out. "Eat up. I've got something special planned for later on." She reached over with her free hand and cranked up the volume. "Who likes sausage rolls?" she shouted, rolling her hips in time to the music.

"People are strange," Morrison chanted, "when you're a stranger."

CHAPTER EIGHTEEN

Moo's "something special" was a teacup reading for each of us. She whispered it to me, when I went into the kitchen to get more potato crisps. She was filling the kettle.

"I thought you weren't going to do this anymore," I said. "Predict the future. Anyone's."

"I've been talking to Pearl about it. I had to tell her I felt responsible."

"It wasn't you, Moo. You know that." I squeezed the air-filled plastic bag of crisps, then lifted it to my teeth to tear open the corner.

"I know that now. She told me that nothing anyone said or did has made any difference for a long time."

"Nothing anyone said? Did she use those words?"

"Yes." Her face softened even more, although I didn't think that was possible. "Go back to your friends. I'll call you when I'm ready."

When she did call us all into the kitchen, I saw that she had cleared off the table, and in the middle was an empty wine bottle with a tall purple candle stuck in the top. She had made a big pot of tea, and it sat on the table, too. Plain white cups and saucers, the ones she kept specifically for tea reading, were piled beside the teapot. She sipped from her glass as she pulled out the four chairs and arranged her Own seat — the stool from Pearl's bedroom — at one end of the table.

"Everyone sit down," she said. "In order for me to read your leaves, you all have to drink a cup of tea. I'm using my very favourite tea for this reading because the leaves make spectacular pictures." She picked up the heavy, plain brown teapot and began pouring; clear, steaming liquid splashed into the first cup. "It's called *Bojenmi.*"

"Reminds me of *Jumanji,*" Andrea said, smiling at me. She was still carrying on with the innocent act.

Moo held the cup under her nose and breathed. "Ah. It smells of sandalwood." She passed it to Kiera, perched on the edge of the chair beside her. "You really shouldn't put any milk or sugar in it," Moo added. "It can affect the outcome."

I looked around the kitchen, seeing it through four fresh pairs of eyes. There was a stack of dirty dishes in the sink, and a pot with dried mashed potatoes stuck to the sides was sitting on the stove. The windowsill over the sink was lined with junk: an almost-empty plastic bottle of dish-washing liquid, a pickle jar filled with broken pencils and leaky ballpoint pens, a chipped ceramic duck that I'd given to Pearl for Christmas when I was about ten, and a good-sized terracotta flowerpot with no plant, just dirt. The speckled beige floor was grimy-looking, and the linoleum in front of the sink was almost worn away. The avocado-coloured fridge hummed noisily. I leaned against it.

Each time Moo finished filling one cup, she slopped a small pool of tea on to the table when she moved the teapot to the next cup. She passed the cups all around. The fifth — mine — was still sitting in front of her.

"No sugar?" asked Miki, lifting her cup and sniffing it.

"I don't like tea," Elsbeth said.

"Go on, girls. Drink as much as you can, without getting the tea leaves in your mouth."

Elsbeth took a sip. "Oooh. It tastes like mud." She made a coughing noise.

"It's not that bad," Kiera said. "Shut up, Elsbeth."

Miki and Andrea didn't say anything, just drank.

I heard the record stop, and the next one drop down from the shaft where I had piled four of them. Now Carol King was singing that she felt the earth move under her feet. Moo hummed along, an ice cube from her drink between her front teeth. She took off the birthday hat and put it on the table beside her glass.

"When it's your turn," Moo said, shifting the ice cube to her cheek, so that it bulged there, "I want you to turn your cup three times." Her voice got lower, the way it always did when she switched into her working technique.

"Does it matter which way?" Andrea asked.

"If you're right-handed, counterclockwise. If you're a lefty, clockwise."

Everyone was watching and listening.

"Then, carefully turn the cup upside down on to the saucer. Place both hands on the bottom of the cup and make a wish. When you've made your wish, remove your hands and don't touch the cup again.

That's when I pick it up and see what stories your leaves have made for you."

There was a moment of silence. Moo could be convincing when she wanted to be.

"How do you know how to do all this?" Kiera asked. She took an elastic out of her pocket and pulled her long, walnut-coloured hair into a thick ponytail.

"It's my job. I tell futures."

"People pay you? To look into their teacups?" The elastic snapped around her hair. There was a half smile on her mouth.

"Yes. I read tarot cards. Palms. I know how to read the future in many different ways." Moo gently rubbed her hands together, as if she were warming them.

"How do you know how to do it?"

"I've always had a sixth sense," Moo said. She took another drink. "Even when I was a girl, I could tell things about people. Just by looking at them." Her eyes bored into Kiera, and Kiera squirmed in her chair after a few seconds.

"Did you go to, like, a future school or anything?" Miki asked. "Or maybe a Future Shop?" She smiled at her own joke, then took a mouthful of tea and wrinkled her nose as she swallowed.

"I've been studying various methods, reading on my own, asking other readers for advice, most of my adult life. My mother read, too. She got me started when I was younger than all of you. And I took a cosmology course once," Moo went on. "That helped me to understand different areas of the craft."

"That's what I want to do," Elsbeth said. "Learn

about all the types of skin, and how to put on make-up properly."

"That's cosmetology, Elsbeth," I said. "Not cosmology. Cosmology is learning about the universe — the stars and planets. How their movements and actions create other actions. How action equals reaction."

"Whatever," Elsbeth said, lifting her cup and drinking without stopping. When she'd finished, gasping, she set her cup in her saucer.

"Is everyone ready?" Moo asked. "Alright. I need a little atmosphere." She took a fluorescent green plastic lighter from the pocket of her caftan and lit the tall purple candle.

Kiera watched her. "Uh, Moo? A minute ago you said "craft"? That the course you took helped you understand the craft. This isn't like that movie, *The Craft,* is it? You know the one? Where those girls make themselves into witches, and do all this freaky stuff? And try to get that other girl to be one of them, too." She looked at me.

"No, it isn't like the movie at all," I said. "It's just tea leaves. It's not like Moo's casting a spell or anything." Kiera was still looking at me. "Why? Do you think I'm a witch?"

Kiera lowered her eyes.

"How come you're not drinking any tea then?" Elsbeth asked. Before I could answer, she went on, quickly, "She didn't drink any of the tea." She looked around the table. "And neither did her aunt." Her eyes skimmed over the thick glass in Moo's hand, then her eyelashes fluttered really quickly, almost an involuntary tic.

"Just stop it, Elsbeth," Andrea said. "You're

always doing that. Getting all worked up over nothing."

I went and took the last cup from the table. "Watch me, Elsbeth." I put the cooling liquid to my lips. "Here I go. I'm drinking. I'm drinking my tea." I gulped it down, then picked a tea leaf off my top lip. I'd swallowed some of the leaves, and they felt sharp, and huge, in my throat. There were still some on my tongue. "Okay. Now, whatever scary thing happens to the rest of you will happen to me, too. I drank the potion."

"Cut it out," Andrea said. "You're both being stupid."

I swallowed again, trying to get the last of the tea leaves down. "I didn't drink my tea because Moo reads my leaves all the time," I said. "I pretty well know my future until I'm a dried-up old prune."

"That's not how it works, Mercy, and you know it," Moo said. "Tea leaves only work on the immediate future."

"How can a future be immediate, if it's in the future?" Andrea asked. "That's like one of those phrases — I forget what they're called — when the two words are opposite. Like jumbo shrimp, or bittersweet," she added.

"I know! I know what those are called," Elsbeth said, waving one hand in the air. "We learned it in English. They're antonyms."

"No, they're not,"Miki said. "They're something else."

"Oxymoron," I said. "And I know, Moo. The immediate future just means it's your future for this week, or maybe the next month, or whatever. Not your whole future. Because that's always changing." I looked into my empty cup, a tiny trail up one side where I'd tipped it to my lips. I put it back on the table. "If Moo read your cup or your cards today, they would be different than what she would read tomorrow, or next week, or next month. Even the lines of your palm could change, depending on how you're feeling and what's happening to you. But your palm doesn't so much tell the future; it shows what kind of person you are."

"But you can change yourself," Andrea said. "You can make yourself into something else; stop being one way and try hard to be another. So maybe even what your palm says isn't necessarily true."

Moo held up her right hand. "I changed mine, by accident. Look." Everybody's head turned toward Moo's upheld hand. The gash had sealed together, but there was still an angry red welt. It ran vertically, right through the middle of her palm. "These are the three main lines," she said, pointing to them. "The one right under your fingers is your heart line. The one under it is your head line. And this other one, sort of curving away from your thumb, is your life line. So I changed things," she said. "I accidentally cut through my heart and head lines. So now there are some breaks in those lines that weren't there before."

"What does that mean?" Kiera asked.

"Actually, breaks in both those lines mean the same thing. A gap in the heart line means that the flow of love in my life isn't going to be even and steady. It's like I'm going to be robbed of the love I deserve. And even a gap in the head line means you'll experience a disappointment of the heart. Not a very good outlook." Her eyes glistened.

Elsbeth leaned forward, licking her lips. "At least you didn't cut your life line. Would that mean you were going to die soon, or something?"

"God, Elsbeth," Miki said. "Would you just shut up, for once?"

"No. It wouldn't mean that. A break in the life line just means that things are ..." Moo hesitated, and looked down at her palm again, "sort of colourless, cheerless. And that it's up to you to take on a new outlook." She'd lost her strong, fortune-telling voice, and had slipped into a quiet, meek one.

I felt a sudden rush of feeling for her. Pity, maybe. She'd gone to a lot of trouble to do this for me, put on this party, and all I felt was embarrassed and angry. I went to her side and took her big hand in mine and studied it. I hadn't held it for a long time. It was soft, with a padded, comforting feel. I suddenly thought of her holding my hand when she took me to the library, all those years ago. She had never let it go, all the way there and all the way back.

"Are you sure?" I asked. "Maybe the breaks you created just indicate what's already behind you. The past. Maybe you're just seeing all the things that have already happened. And as your hand heals more, with more time, the scar will fade. Like pain does."

Moo put her other hand over mine and lowered her head.

Oh, no. Please don't start crying, Moo. Not now. Not only because it would be bad enough if Moo started bawling in the middle of the party, but also because I felt suspiciously close to crying, too. Since I'd cried in the hospital, it seemed like the tears had never quite gone away from beneath my eyelids.

But in the next second she raised her head and smiled at all the faces around the table. "Now, wouldn't you say my niece has inherited a bit of the visionary?" Her voice was robust again. "It's handed down in families, you know. I got it from my mother, and she got it from her mother. That's how it works, these gifts. They run in the genes." She looked up at me, and patted my hand with her top one, squeezing it with her bottom one at the same time. Then she opened both her hands to release mine. I left it there for one extra heartbeat.

"Read mine first, okay, Mrs ..., um, ... okay, Moo?" Kiera said, sliding her cup and saucer forward.

"Yes," Moo said. "Let's get started."

CHAPTER NINETEEN

❦

It was pretty typical, as far as Moo's readings go. Everybody was happy about something. She told Kiera that she saw a rooster. That meant Kiera would have something to crow about; she would be proud of some accomplishment.

"That's my driving test, next week. I'm going to pass for sure," Kiera said, leaning forward, holding her ponytail with one hand as she wriggled closer to Moo on her chair.

"And there's a lovely little moon," Moo went on. "A moon always indicates romance."

For Miki, there was money everywhere. "Look at all these groups of three dots," Moo said. "Are you expecting an inheritance?"

"No," Miki said, laughing. "Maybe my parents are finally going to up my allowance."

"And look at this. An S. Does that letter have any significance for you?"

Elsbeth and Kiera squealed. "Stefan!" Kiera shouted. "I told you he's been watching you, Miki."

Moo studied Elsbeth's. "There's a journey coming up for you. See that bear? It won't be far, but it will be somewhere you hoped to go."

"My swim team is competing in Brandon next month. Could that be it?"

"It might be. Oh, and look at this," Moo said.

"What?" Elsbeth put her hand to her mouth.

"There's a little diamond. Look, right there. Do you see it?"

Elsbeth squinted. "Yeah. Yeah, I can see it. Is that something awful?"

"No. It means you'll be getting a gift."

Elsbeth's face brightened even more.

But it was Andrea who seemed the most thrilled.

"Your cup is very, very, positive," Moo told her, after studying the cup for a few minutes, then turning it to one side and pointing in to show Andrea. "There's a closed circle, right there. That means there will be some form of completion in your life, something that might have felt unfinished, or missing, before."

Andrea put both hands against her chest, over her heart.

"And see here — a fish. A fish in a cup is a wonderful sign."

"What does it mean?" Andrea's eyes were huge and shining.

"It means that a wish is going to come true," Moo told her.

"It does?" Andrea said, glancing at me. I told you, her glance said.

All the girls were laughing and talking about the predictions.

Moo smiled at me. "Time for cake," she said, getting up and taking the terracotta flowerpot from the windowsill. The cake had been sitting in front of us the whole time. "A special mud cake for Mercy because she spends half her life with flowers and pots and compost, at her job," Moo said. She set the pot beside the wine bottle. "We have some clean plates somewhere."

"I'll find them," I said, opening a cupboard. Mud cake — the gooey, chocolate mess that was half cake, half pudding. I had loved it when I was about six. And Moo had made it again. Come to think of it, it was the only cake I'd ever known Moo to make. She had left all the baking to my mother. Pearl had created some really beautiful birthday cakes, for both Moo and me, over the years. Not last year, though. She'd bought me an ice cream cake from Dairy Queen for my fifteenth birthday. I suddenly remembered how disappointed I'd been, but I hadn't asked her why she didn't make me one, and she hadn't offered any excuses. I handed Moo a big spoon and the plates.

She took them, looked at the cake, and wailed. "I forgot to get candles!"

"It doesn't matter," I said.

"Here," Moo said, grabbing the burning purple candle out of the wine bottle. She stuck it into the top of the cake. "Let's sing."

She started singing "Happy Birthday," and everyone joined in. I looked at their faces as they were singing. They were all looking back at me. And they were smiling. Not that trying-too-hard smile that kids, or teachers, or guidance counsellors often gave me. These seemed to be real smiles. I smiled back, then blew out the candle, and Moo clapped.

"I hope you get your wish, sweetheart," she said, digging into the pot and spooning out a slippery mound. "First piece to the birthday girl. Look out, Mercy — there's a big worm!"

I pulled the red gummy worm out of the chocolate. Putting my head back, I held the worm over my open mouth and then dropped it in. I did it for Moo. I couldn't imagine trying to get it down my throat, which felt like it had shrunken to the size of a thread.

"Ewww. Gross," Miki said. "Can I get one?"

"Sure," Moo said. "There's lots. I put in a whole package."

When no one was looking I took the worm out of my mouth and put it in the garbage under the sink. In a few minutes everyone was laughing and pulling the worms out of their cake and talking and eating. There was no more music; the last record had dropped and played while Moo was still reading the cups.

"Can I have some more, please?" Kiera asked. As she passed her plate to Moo, she turned to me. "It's too bad your mom couldn't be here. For your birthday."

Moo was wrestling with the spoon.

"Yeah," I said.

"Is she coming home soon?" Miki scraped at her plate with her spoon, then scooped up the last wet bits and put them in her mouth. "What's wrong with her anyway?" she asked, casually. I realized it was a casual question. A normal question.

I opened my mouth, but nothing came out. *My mother is,* my voice repeated in my head, *my mother is,* at first loud, and then softer and softer, *my mother, my mother, my mother.* If my voice could have had a shape, it would have looked like what you see if you hold a mirror up to another mirror — that identical image of yourself holding a mirror, growing smaller and smaller until finally it's nothing more than a dot.

I closed my mouth.

"I told you, Miki," Andrea said. "She's in the hospital. She has to have some check-ups and stuff." She said it like she knew my mother, like she'd actually seen her, talked to her. Like I'd told her that — my mother has to have some things checked out. She looked at me. "This has really been fun, Mercy," she said.

"Thanks." *Thank you, Andrea,* I thought.

"Yeah, thanks Mercy, thanks Moo," Elsbeth said. "Could you look at my palm sometime, and tell me what you see?" she asked Moo. "I could go to where you work."

"Oh, you don't have to go there and pay me. You could walk home with Mercy after school someday, and I'll do it here. Or I could read your tarot cards."

"Me, too?" Kiera said.

"Ditto," Miki said.

"Anytime," Moo told them, smiling broadly. "I've got all the time in the world for Mercy's friends." She picked up the cup in front of her and glanced at it. "I didn't read this one." Her neck twisted so that she could see me. "Is it yours?"

I nodded.

"Well, look at that!" She turned my cup so everyone could see it. "This is one of the best possible signs," she said. "A bird in the cup is very good luck. But, Mercy, you've got so many — more than a dozen, I bet. You've got a whole flock of birds in your cup, Mercy. You're so, so lucky! "

CHAPTER TWENTY

❦

The girls had left, the flowerpot of cake empty, the dirty dishes piled on the counter, but Moo and I were still sitting at the kitchen table. Moo was eating the last bit of cake. My presents were spread out in front of me. There was a journal with a beautiful cover from Elsbeth, a bracelet made of little silvery loops from Kiera, a square green candle in a black metal candleholder that had little stars punched out all around it from Miki, and a white ceramic picture frame with the word "Friends" spelled across the bottom in tiny red shiny beads from Andrea.

"I didn't have a picture of us together to put in it," Andrea had said when I'd unwrapped it. "But next time you come over, I'll get my mom to take one of us. If you want to, that is," she added.

"Sure," I'd said.

I ran my hand over the sweater sitting in the open box. It was from Moo and Pearl. "Pearl said it would be beautiful on you," Moo had told me. "She saw it in a flyer last month, and I went down and picked it up." The sweater was thin, soft wool, the colour of melted caramel. "She said it would match your eyes perfectly."

"I like your friends," Moo told me now. She took another long drink. I'd stopped counting after her fourth glass. Her words were slow and careful, and her eyes were slits of blue. "They're nice girls." She picked up the stub of the purple candle, its base smeared with chocolate.

"Will your wish come true, Mercy? I hope your wish comes true. Remember the birds in your cup. They're such good luck."

I felt as if I were part of someone else's dream, as if the kitchen were saturated with bright yellow dye. I closed my eyes to shut it out, and suddenly I had to lean forward, put my head on the table. There was noise, and it seemed as if it were white, rushing in my ears. I never knew noise could be so bright.

"Mercy?" The voice came from far away. "You sleeping, baby girl?"

I tried to lift my head, but it took too much effort. "I have to go to bed," I said to the table.

"Stay up with me. Have some more cake. Oh, there isn't any more. Did you have cake? I don't think you had cake. How come you didn't have cake?" Moo's voice faded in and out, growing louder and softer, with a throb of its own. "Because it wasn't good? I know, Merce, I know; your mom wasn't here to bake you a cake. We need her cake, don't we, Merce?" I knew Moo was crying. "And I don't know where Barry is. He promised me he'd be back, weeks ago. And he's still not here. Where's Barry, Mercy?"

I weakly pushed my chair back from the table, half raising my head at the same time.

"Was it a nice party?" Moo sobbed. "Did I do good?"

I could see the floor under the table. The specks in the linoleum seemed to be dancing; tiny bugs whirling and jumping in step to some beat, the same beat as the one in my head, as Moo's voice. "I think it was a nice party," her voice went on. "Want to know something? I told your mother, I told her, 'That girl needs a party.' 'She won't like it,' Pearl said, 'she won't like it,' but I said, 'I know Mercy, and I think she needs a party.' I said that to her in the hospital. 'That girl needs some cheering up'." I brought my eyes up to meet the voice. Moo lifted her glass. Her cheeks were a wet blur of blue and black streaks. "So, Mercy, cheers," and she drank again.

I wanted to say something to her about the party something — but it seemed too overwhelming an effort.

Somehow I got down the hall, but I don't remember doing it. I don't remember pulling down the rope, or getting up the narrow, steep steps to my bed, but I can remember how cool the pillow felt under my cheek, and my head hurting so much, and wondering if this was how Pearl remembered things.

I might have slept. Figures swirled under my eyelids, red against black, black against red, faces and flowers and birds that grew as if they were fire burning through black paper. I was hot, too hot, and so thirsty. I wanted something to drink; the need was so strong that I turned my head in the dim light, and could make out the shadowy shape of the flowers on my desk. I wanted to drink the scummy green water in the mayonnaise jar.

As I watched the outline of the flowers, it grew, slowly but steadily, into a huge and menacing head with an open mouth. B's head. I whimpered, and squeezed my eyes shut, rolling off the mattress to get away, rolling on to the floor with a thump. I thought I heard a series of echoing thumps, and I imagined that Moo must have rolled out of bed on to the floor, too, and then Pearl. We were all rolling out of bed, all hitting the floor at the same time. We were all sick.

No. Pearl wasn't here.

Get up, I told myself. *Go downstairs and get a glass of water.* And then, as if for once I could actually make a wish come true just by trying hard enough, I was downstairs, at the bottom of the steps, sprawled against the last one. In the light that shone from the kitchen, I saw my legs sticking out in front of me, and I wondered why I still had on my black tights and skirt, why I wasn't in the T-shirt and sweatpants I always wore to bed. That's why I was so cold. No, that's why I was so hot. I was hot, and I was shivering.

I closed my eyes again, and heard loud, rustling noises, like heavy-footed animals running through a field of dry grass. And then there was a long, drawn-out cry, and voices — two garbled voices.

I opened my eyes. "Who is it?" I heard myself ask.

A woman was standing in front of me. She was short and square, reminding me of Mama Gio, but only her shape was the same. Where Mama Gio was a plain little grackle, this woman was a luxuriant bird-of-paradise. Her long, down-filled coat was bright turquoise, and the scarf tied in a big knot at her throat was pink. A red and green plaid hat with a rolled brim was pulled low on her forehead. Her mittens looked like they'd been knitted from leftover scraps of wool — stripe after stripe of different colours, pink and green and blue and brown. She carried a flowered suitcase in one hand, and a plastic Sears bag and another bag made of heavy string in the other.

"Who is it?" I asked, again.

Moo was standing behind her, although I hadn't seen her at first. "Good Lord, Mercy. What happened?"

"Who is that? Her," I said, pointing to the image in I front of me. When I lifted my arm it felt as if my bones and muscles had been replaced with rubbery jelly.

Moo shook her head. "It's the Queen of Cups," she said. "The Queen of Cups." She rubbed her hand over her lips. "I can't take anything more tonight. I need a drink. Jesus, Mary, and Joseph, I need a drink."

"Drink," I echoed, and closed my eyes.

CHAPTER TWENTY-ONE

❦

The next time I woke up I was on the couch. There was a sheet under me, my pillow under my head, and my quilt covering me from my feet to my waist. As I adjusted my eyes to the light, my hand reached down and stroked the quilt.

"You're finally awake," a voice said.

It hadn't been part of the dream. The woman was there, in the chair by the window. She wasn't wearing the coat and hat and scarf and mitts, but was still in bright colours. A wool sweater, knitted in a wavy pattern of dark blue and light blue. A pair of stretchy red trousers. Thick yellow socks. Her hair was short and a washed-out red-grey frizz. A stretchy black hair band pulled it away from her forehead.

She got up and came toward me. I tugged the quilt up to my chin. She didn't seem to notice that I was trying to pull away from her, and she put her hand on my forehead. "Still high," she said, "but not as bad as before. You were burning up last night. Delirious, muttering and fussing. I forced you to take a few pills to get the fever down. You weren't very co-operative."

I saw a big bowl of water on the coffee table. A wrung-out washcloth was neatly folded and hung over one side of the bowl. I had a dreamy memory of cool dampness on my forehead and cheeks and neck.

"Goodness, girl, I'm not going to bite." She went back to the chair and picked up the Sears bag. She took a scratched brown leather purse out of it. When she put the plastic bag down again, it made the same rustling sound as I'd heard the night before, too loud, hurting my ears.

"I never carry my purse in the open," she said, undoing the clasp. "Invites trouble." She dug around inside her purse, finally pulling out a plastic bottle of white tablets. "I want you to take two of these." She shook the bottle over her palm, then came back to me. "Sit up, now." She put one short, strong arm around my shoulders and dragged me into a half-sitting position. "Here." She held out the pills.

"What are they?" I asked. My tongue felt like a piece of driftwood, catching the words and slowing them down before they got to my lips.

"Just plain old aspirin. And here's some water. Take a sip of water first, then swallow these down."

I kept looking at the pills. "Where's Moo?"

"Maureen's sleeping it off, I expect. Luckily she was still up when I got here, late last night. If Maureen had been passed out, and you in the state you were in, I could have pounded on the door until I broke my hand for all the good it would have done me, trying to get in.

"I didn't expect to be so late; the bus had trouble on the road and didn't pull in to the depot until after ten, instead of eight. Then I had to get from the depot over here." She shook her head. "These old bones are pretty stiff this morning, after the long bus trip, and this damp weather. You should have seen me climbing up that ladder to get your pillow and quilt! I won't be doing that again. Moo told me to use what was on Pearl's bed, but it didn't look like it had been washed for a long time. And when a body is sick, they like the feel of their own bedding." She stopped for a breath.

"Sitting up in that chair most of the night didn't help my back either." She twisted at the waist, rotating her upper body. "But I figured someone should be watching over you. And Maureen was sure in no shape to look after anyone. I'll get Pearl's things washed today, so I can sleep in her room tonight. And you'll stay down here, where we can keep an eye on you."

She still had her arm around me, was still holding the pills in front of me.

"But who *are* you?" I asked.

She let go of me and eased me back down, looking into my face. "You didn't hear anything of what I told you last night?"

I started to shake my head, then stopped, wincing with both the pain it shot through my temples, and with the vague memory of something Moo had said.

"The Queen of Cups," I said. "Moo said you were the Queen of Cups."

The woman snorted. "I don't know what she was on about; drunk as a skunk, she was. Shameful. And I'm nobody's queen. I'm just your grandma. Your mother called me. Asked me to come."

"Grandma?" I said.

"In the flesh. Come on. Take these; I'm not going to hold on to them all day."

Squinting against the pain, I drank from the glass the woman, who said she was my grandmother, was holding, then took the two small white tablets from her seamed palm and put them in my mouth, and took another drink of water. The pills seemed to expand in my throat, growing larger and larger each time I tried to swallow them. When they finally found their way down, it felt like I'd swallowed two Ping-Pong balls. I couldn't help moaning. Just a little.

"Now, you close your eyes again, and try to steep. I'll be right here."

I think my head nodded once. I did close my eyes. "Pearl asked you to come for her?" I whispered.

"Nope."

"But I thought you said —"

"She asked me to come. But not for her."

I heard a swoosh as she sat down in the chair again.

"For you. She asked me to come for you. Swallowed her pride, Pearl did, and said it didn't matter anymore what had gone on between her and me. What mattered now was you, she said. You," she repeated.

Again, the rustling grass. The same garbled voices — harsh, whispering. Then I realized I could understand them if I listened hard enough.

"Disgraceful," one voice hissed. "She could have broken her neck, falling down those stairs. Or been lying up in that place that you say is her bedroom, with those awful, plastic ripped walls, half dead with fever. And you would never have been the wiser."

"I'm sorry, Ma," the other voice whispered. "I didn't know she was sick."

"That's just what I mean. How could you, if you don't know what's going on right in front of you?"

"But she could have told me. She didn't tell me there was anything wrong last night." The voice was hoarse, ragged, as if it had been swallowing tiny shards of glass. Exactly what mine felt like.

"Oh, keep quiet. You were always the one for excuses, blaming everyone else," the angry voice rasped.

Yes, quiet, I thought. *Keep quiet.* The pounding in my head got louder and louder, until all I could hear was the dull thud, thud, thud of a far-off hammer. *Quiet, all of you.*

CHAPTER TWENTY-TWO

❦

I felt a hand rest against my cheek for a brief moment, and lifted my heavy eyelids.

"How are you feeling?"

I tried to unstick my eyelashes. "I don't know," I mumbled.

"Ma says you should take some more of these. It's been over four hours," Moo said. She opened her hand in front of my eyes, and I saw two more of the disguised ping-pong balls.

"Okay," I said, carefully sitting up. They had helped. At least the hammer and rustling grass and voices were gone, and I knew I'd been in a deep sleep. I took a sip of water, put the pills into my mouth and drained the glass, trying not to groan. Then I gingerly lowered my head on to the pillow. A shaft of weak sunlight coming through the curtains stabbed my eyes. I turned my head away.

"What time is it?"

"Almost eleven," Moo said.

"Oh, no! I was supposed to be at work an hour ago. I promised Vince I'd be there."

"You're not going."

"I can't miss any more. Phone him, Moo. Tell him I'll be in later; tell him I'm sick, but I'll be in." Everything was going wrong. Everything. "Or maybe just phone him and tell him I quit, to save him the trouble of firing me." I moved forward, rocking to get myself up. My head almost exploded. "No. Don't phone him. I'll go to work."

"I'll call him and tell him you've got a high fever. He can't fire you over being sick. You're not going anywhere."

I knew she was right. I knew I'd never even make it back up the steps to my room to get changed. I closed my eyes. "But Vince has been so good to me. Will you make sure he knows I'm really sick? That I'm sorry?"

There was a moment of silence, and then I sensed Moo moving away from me. "Will you call him?" I asked again.

"Yes," Moo answered. She sighed. I suddenly remembered what I'd wanted to say to her last night, after the party. "And Moo?"

Her footsteps stopped.

"Thanks for last night. It was a super party. It really was," I repeated, opening my eyes.

Moo gave me a small, sad smile, and then left.

By late afternoon I felt well enough to take a bath. When I came out, shaky and light-headed, wrapped in Pearl's old flannel housecoat, there was a plate of buttered toast and a cup of hot chocolate on the coffee table.

"Try to have a few bites to eat," Grandma said, from the chair in the corner. "You look hollowed out."

I sat down on the couch, noticing that the sheets

had been straightened and the quilt neatly pulled up. "We didn't have any cocoa left," I said.

"Didn't have much of anything, from what I could see," Grandma said. "This morning, while you were sleeping, I went to that shop a few blocks down and bought a few basics. We'll have to see about getting in some proper food later on. Do you want jam with your toast? I bought strawberry."

I shook my head. "I don't really know if I can eat anything." The smell of the hot chocolate was good warm and sweet. I was hungry, but if the pills and water were any indication, I knew it would be torture to try to eat any real food.

"You just take your time." She stood up. "Do you think it's just a flu? Or is there anything else that's hurting? Last night I was worried about your appendix. That happened to Pearl, when she was about twelve. Awful fever, and the pain in her side. She had to have it out, the appendix. I kept asking you, last night, if you had a pain in your side, and you kept saying no, so I took it that it wasn't your appendix."

"It really hurts when I try to swallow. Like there's a great big burning lump."

"Could be strep throat. You should see a doctor."

"There's a walk-in clinic not too far from here. If it's still like this tomorrow, I'll go."

Grandma nodded. "Well, now that I can see you're in better shape, I'm going over to the hospital and visit Pearl." She smoothed her sweater over her wide hips.

I couldn't see much of a resemblance to either Pearl or Moo in this woman, who was my grandmother. She didn't look like those old pictures anymore either. Even her crooked teeth had been replaced by straight, gleaming dentures. "How long has it been? Since you've seen her? Pearl?"

"Last time was when she was about your age," she said.

"Sixteen? You haven't seen her since she was sixteen?"

Grandma got up. "Not because I didn't want to." She paused. "Pearl never told you about it?"

I shook my head.

"Then it's not up to me. All I'll say is that when I left, she and her sister decided to stay with their father. I figured they were old enough to make that decision. Maureen and I have kept in touch. But your mother, well, it seems she gave up on me."

"Why?"

"Because I wasn't what she thought I should be. Wouldn't give me a second chance." Her lips tightened suddenly. "There I go, talking too much. I said I wouldn't." She looked toward the hall. "Was that a knock?"

"I didn't hear anything."

She went into the kitchen, and I heard the back door rasp. Then I heard her voice, and Moo's, and a man's. I pulled the quilt over my shoulders and closed my eyes, the red and black starting to dance against my lids again. I heard the back door complain a second time.

"Your boss is here," Moo said.

"Did he come to check on me? To see if I really am sick? Or just to tell me I'm fired?" Then I opened my eyes and saw that Moo was holding a potted azalea.

It was covered with delicate flowers, a soft, pinky-white.

"This is for you," she said, "from him." Her voice lowered. "Is his name Vic?"

"Vince," I said, reaching toward the plant as Moo set it beside the toast on the table. I felt the satin of one of the petals between my fingers. "Why did he bring this for me?"

"I don't know. He just showed up at the door and handed the plant to me and said, 'Tell Mercy I hope she gets better soon.' I'd better go back," Moo said, in that same starchy whisper. "He's just standing there. You know, he looks very familiar."

"He drove me to the hospital. He was there, in Emergency. Maybe you saw him."

Moo nodded. "That would be it. Now Ma's gone off to the hospital. That Vic, or Vince, said he'd drive her, but she wouldn't hear of it. She's like that. Doesn't trust people." She left me alone, and I heard her voice for a while, and the low rumble that was Vince's.

I could feel myself floating along the thin rope between wake and sleep. Just as I was about to let myself go — slide down into the beckoning dark — Moo's voice got louder, and I climbed up the rope and listened.

"And yours are quite something. I can't help but notice, because of my job. Do you mind if I have a look?"

Don't tell me Moo was looking at Vince's hands. God, what would he think of my family? It had been so safe, before, at the shop, where there were just beautiful flowers and living green plants and the sounds of opera and the smell of fresh coffee. He hadn't asked anything about me, apart from that first day and the talk about names. I did whatever he asked, ate home-made goodies from the seemingly bottomless plastic container, and went home when he locked up.

Then everything changed: the jumbled phone call from Moo, the careening drive to the hospital, and now this my long-lost and apparently suspicious grandmother in her peacock clothes, and Moo in her caftan and turban, hung-over and holding his hand.

I'd never find another job as good as the one at Santa Marie Florist, I thought. *How could he want me to work there, knowing all this about me?*

"I'd love to do a reading sometime. Your hands are ... well, I've never seen a hand with so *much.*" *Oh, Moo.*

"So much what?"

"Let's put it this way," Moo answered, "some hands are like those paperback romances. You know, a standard plot and predictable characters and a sure thing at the end. You can pretty well anticipate what will happen right from the first five pages. Other hands are like ..." I could see Moo looking up at the ceiling, her lips gathered like a drawstring bag as she thought. "*Anna Karenina.* Or *Dr Zhivago.* One of those huge long classics that take all sorts of twists and turns and you're always surprised. And you can't stop thinking about them once you've finished them."

I wondered if she was still holding on to his giant hand.

"*I read Gone With the Wind,*" Vince said. "A long time ago. It was like that."

"Well, there you go," Moo answered, and I could hear the smile in her voice. "Your palm is definitely the *Gone-With-the-Wind* type."

"I never read those other books, but I rented *Dr Zhivago* a few months ago. Watched it twice; I liked it. The music, too."

The rope was tempting me again. This time I went with it.

❦

It seemed I woke up and fell asleep and woke up all day. The next time I stirred, I saw Moo sitting in the chair by the window.

"That was kind of him," she said, her eyes on the plant, reaching up to wipe her mouth with her hand like she did when she was thinking about having a drink. Her lips looked as dry as mine felt.

"Yeah. He's a nice man," I said.

Moo kept looking at the plant. "There aren't many men left who bring flowers around."

"He knows I like these," I said. "And Vince is like that." My voice was as raspy as the back door.

"No. Not many who bring flowers," Moo repeated. "Or who keep their promises. Show up when they're supposed to."

I knew what she was talking about. I hadn't told her about B phoning yesterday.

Moo came over to the table, bent down, and put her nose to the plant. When she stood up, she said, "I'm sorry you're sick, Mercy."

"It's okay."

"You weren't sick at your party, were you? You seemed to be having a good time."

"I felt horrible." Her face sagged. "But I still had a good time," I half-lied. She had tried so hard. "It's okay, Moo. Don't worry about it."

"But I should have realized something was wrong," she said. I saw her eyes move to the cold dried toast, the still full mug with a thick, dark skin floating on the top.

She didn't say any more, but that last sentence was the same thing she'd said about Pearl, back in the Emergency room. *I should have realized something was wrong.*

I sat up. I heard myself saying, "It's okay," over and over to her. I was always saying, "It's okay." But it really wasn't. "It's hard to realize things when you're drunk, Moo." Maybe it was because my throat was so sore, or because my brain had this heavy, veiled feeling that also blocked my ears, but my voice didn't sound like my own. It wasn't like the raging monster voice from the hospital, but something slow, and hard. Mean.

Her eyes widened, and she put her hand up to her lips again. Her fingers were trembling.

There. I'd said it. Drunk. Moo was a drunk. Grandma had said it so easily. *Why didn't I say anything before? Why didn't Pearl?* Moo's drinking wasn't a secret; she didn't try to hide it, and yet all three of us carefully avoided it, just like we carefully avoided talking about what had been happening to Pearl for a long time. Her slipping into black nothingness — her depression. Just like I didn't tell about B. All these secrets that kept getting bigger and bigger, that grew, alone, in darkness, like the plant tubers Vince had shown me. They were ugly, twisted roots that you kept in soil, in a dark, cool spot. You didn't bring them into the light, and yet they stayed alive, growing, getting bigger and stronger.

"So don't you worry about anything," I went on, in that terrible, unfamiliar voice. "Grandma's here. She's looking after me right now. Pearl's in the hospital, all safe and sound with the nurses and doctors. She can go away into her private world anytime she wants. And you can go to yours, Moo. You can drink all you like, without having to worry about one single goddamned thing. Not that you really did, anyway. And pretty soon your boyfriend will be back. Anytime. He phoned, you know. He phoned yesterday."

Moo sat up straight. "Yesterday? Did he say he was coming?"

"Yeah. Any day now. But I didn't get around to telling you. So now your life will be complete, won't it? Barry will be back, and you still won't realize that anything is wrong, will you?" I heard what I was saying. *Don't stop,* I told myself. *Now. Tell her.*

"What do you mean? I could see that you didn't like him, but you hardly like anyone. So I didn't pay any attention. I thought you'd get over it."

"Get over it? Didn't you ever wonder why, though? Why I wouldn't even talk to him? Why I wouldn't ever go anywhere with him? Why I stayed in that hot, jammed little bedroom with Pearl every night? Didn't you ever see him—"

"Maureen! Maureen, get yourself out here!" It was

Grandma, hollering from the back door. "I stopped to shop on the way home from the hospital. I've got a taxi filled with groceries. Come help me haul them in."

Moo was staring at me. "I'll be back after I help Ma."

"Never mind," I said. "Just never mind." I lay down and pulled the quilt over my shoulders again. I kept my eyes closed tight, so I wouldn't have to see that strange, blank look on Moo's face. Like she didn't have a clue what was going on. She would never believe it, even if I did tell her.

Again, I thought of those few awful minutes in the Emergency room. Moo's face looked the same as it did the day Pearl had almost died.

CHAPTER TWENTY-THREE

❦

I was still shaky and tired on Sunday morning. As long as I took a couple of pills every three or four hours, I didn't feel like I'd been punched in the head by a huge boxing glove. I still had a fever, but it was low. The worst thing was my throat; I could barely even swallow my own saliva.

Grandma kept fluttering around me. I knew that both she and Moo had each checked on me once in the night. I'd woken enough to hear them cross the living room and stand over me, pressing a hand against my cheek or forehead. "I'm alright," I had mumbled each time.

"I'm going with you to that walk-in clinic," she said. "You should have a swab of your throat taken. If it is strep, you won't get better for quite a while without antibiotics. I'll call a cab, and we'll go over there right now."

"It's too expensive," I said. "A cab."

"For whom? Did I say I couldn't afford a cab? And you're not in any state to be walking anywhere, or waiting for buses."

I picked at the fraying hem of the bathrobe.

"So you go upstairs — careful, mind, you won't be too steady yet — and get dressed. I'll phone for the cab right now, and we'll be off. When we get back, Moo and I are going to the hospital."

I stood up. "You're going to see her again today?"

"Of course." I hadn't asked her about her visit yesterday, and she hadn't mentioned my mother. Not even once.

"Grandma's waiting for you in the cab," I told Moo when I came in from the clinic. "She said to hurry up; the meter's running." I walked by Moo and sat on the couch.

"Okay. We'll be back after we visit with Pearl. We'll stay a few hours; have lunch with her." Moo was fumbling with her purse, pulling at the buttons on her coat. It seemed like she didn't want to look at me. "And when we come back, I want you to finish telling me what you were saying yesterday."

I got up and turned on the television. It was a wildlife show; white birds hopping around on the back of a rhinoceros on some dusty African plain.

"Alright, Mercy?" She looked toward the window as two short, hard horn blasts sounded from the taxi outside.

"The meter's running," I said, staring at the television screen. "Lock the door on your way out."

After I heard the door close, I tried to keep my eyes open, tried to follow the swaying, lumbering stroll of a line of elephants on their way to a water hole, but my eyelids were so heavy.

I think it was the silence that woke me. I woke with a jerk, that stomach-dropping jolt that you feel when you dream that you're stepping off a curb, or stumbling on a step, but I didn't open my eyes. I lay there, in the quiet, and finally opened one eye, and saw the vacant screen. I tried to remember getting up to turn off the television, but couldn't. I looked at my watch. Grandma and Moo had only been gone for about forty-five minutes. As I looked at the blank, square eye of the television, I could see myself on the couch, the flowers from Vince in front of me on the coffee table. I could see part of the room, the chair by the window. And in the chair was B.

I sat up so fast my head threatened to spin off my neck.

"Good morning, Merry Sunshine," he said. "Or good afternoon ."

"How did you get in?" I croaked, pulling at the quilt, holding it up against me.

"Like normal people do," he said, putting his hands on the knees of his jeans. "Through the door. It wasn't locked." He was watching me, not smiling. His dark hair was cut shorter than it used to be. "All the time I was away I was hoping that you had changed your hair back to the way it used to be. I told your mother, just before I left, that she shouldn't have let you do that. It spoils your looks. Why would you do something like that? Get rid of all that pretty hair?"

"My mother can't tell me what to do," I said. "About my hair, or about anything. Nobody can."

He smiled at that, shaking his head. His eyes almost disappeared when he smiled. "Mercy, Mercy,

Mercy. You think you're such a big girl now." He stood, then came toward the couch. "And you haven't even given me a welcome-home hug." He spread his arms wide.

"Get away from me," I said, standing up, too, still holding the quilt around me. I remembered him as being tall. But now I saw that he wasn't much taller than I was.

He took a step back, a put-on look of hurt surprise on his face. "Hey, let's not start off like this. No hard feelings about anything, okay, Mercy? I'm back; I'm family again." He reached into the pocket of his red and black checked shirt. "Look. I brought you a little gift." It was a small, velvet box. He opened it and held it toward me. "I know you like earrings."

They were gold hoops.

"Real gold. Fourteen carat," he said. "I made a bundle on this job. I can buy you lots of pretty things. We can be friends, Mercy, if you just let me. And friends do things for each other. You know the old saying — you scratch my back, I'll scratch yours." He grinned.

"No," I said. "I'll never be your friend. Ever."

"Yes, you will," he said. "We'll go slow. Nice and slow. I'm not such a bad guy. You'll see."

I turned away, the edge of the quilt twirling with me, sweeping against the plant on the coffee table and knocking it to the floor. Dirt spilled out on to the carpet.

"Now look what you did," B said, coming close enough to catch the edge of the quilt.

I didn't even think about what I did next. I didn't plan it, but my hand came up, suddenly, and raked against B's cheek. My fingernails left four raised lines.

He stopped, putting his fingers to his cheek, then took them away and looked at them. One of the lines oozed tiny drops of blood.

I heard the back door open. "Mercy?"

It was Moo. "Mercy?" she called again. "Didn't I lock this door? I had to come back, to —" She had been talking all the way through the kitchen and down the hall. Now she stood in the doorway of the living room. I saw her look at B, standing right in front of me, with his scratched cheek. At the plant, spilled over on the floor. At me, wrapped tightly in the quilt, my whole body shaking.

"Oh, my God," she said. She put both hands up to her own cheeks.

"Hi, baby," B said. "I'm back." He opened his arms, the way he had to me. "You are definitely looking as big and beautiful as you did in all my dreams. Where's my hug?"

CHAPTER TWENTY-FOUR

❦

After that I watched as Moo talked to B, and he talked back. Then she grabbed him by the arm and shook it, and yelled into his face. He yelled back. They yelled for what seemed like a long time, while I just stood there. Why was I having so much trouble understanding everyone? First Moo and Grandma, when I was so sick, and now Moo and B. I was watching their mouths, Moo's and B's, but it seemed like there was some sort of interference, and I couldn't quite catch the words. Their faces were filled with colour: B's a dark, heavy burgundy; Moo's a bright, light pink. She was crying. Then she slapped him — a hard, silent slap, on the same cheek that I'd scratched. She slapped him on the shoulder, and on the chest. He made a fist and pulled it back, and that's when I screamed. I heard the sound my own voice made, as if I'd just come crashing up through a glassy surface, and the sound exploded and fell down around me in shining bright pieces, and then I was standing beside Moo, and I could hear and understand everything again.

B dropped his fist. He looked at me, then back to Moo. "What about my money?" he said to her. "All that money. Everything I paid for? You think it's that simple, that I'm just gonna walk out of here, lose it all? My money, and you, Maureen?"

"We'll pay every cent back. I don't know how, but we will. You give me an address, and I'll mail it to you."

B's lips twisted. "Sure. You'll send me the money."

"We will. You'll see. Just get out, and don't come back." She put her arm around me.

I don't think B really believed Moo until that moment. He tried to touch Moo's face, but she pulled away.

"We had something really good, baby," he said. "And you know it. You're gonna miss me. I don't know what lies she's been telling, but someday you'll be sorry you believed her, and not me."

"Come on, Mercy," Moo said, and pulled me with her, into her bedroom. After she shut the door she collapsed on to the bed, covering her face with her hands. Now she was the one shaking. I sat beside her, listening. Finally I heard the back door slam.

"Do you think he'll come back?" I asked, quietly.

Moo took her hands away from her face. She was still crying, but quietly now. She shook her head. "I think he realizes there's nothing for him here anymore." She wiped her cheeks.

"Why did you come back so soon, Moo? From the hospital?"

"I couldn't stop thinking about what you said, yesterday. Then I told your mother that Barry might arrive today, and she said, 'Is Mercy all alone?' At first I thought she meant because you were sick. I didn't want to believe it could be what I'd started thinking, but I had to come home and ask you, get the truth."

"Are you mad at me, Moo? I know how much you loved him."

Moo squeezed her eyes shut. "Oh, Mercy," was all she said. "Mercy." She picked up my hand and held it tight.

We were still sitting on Moo's bed when Grandma got back.

"What happened to you?" she asked Moo. "You ran out of there like you'd seen a ghost."

"I just realized something," Moo said. "Something really important, and I couldn't stay."

Grandma made a tsking sound. "What could be more important than visiting your own sister in hospital?" But she didn't wait for an answer. "And you, miss," she said, staring at me for a long minute, "you get back to that couch, and rest. You look as though your fever's come back."

The clinic called by noon Monday morning. The results of the swab showed that it was, as Grandma had predicted, strep throat, and the doctor had already phoned in a prescription to the pharmacy nearest us.

"Maureen, you go and pick up the antibiotics right now," Grandma said. "Do you have money?"

Moo dipped her head. "I'm a little short right now."

"There's some on my desk, upstairs," I said.

Grandma picked up her purse. "Here," she said, holding a twenty and a ten out to Moo. "Take this.

Well, what are you waiting for? Get going. The sooner Mercy starts the medication, the sooner it will knock out the bacteria, and her throat can heal."

While Moo was gone, Grandma made some tea. "Can you drink even a bit? I put milk and sugar in it," she said. "I don't know how you can keep going, with nothing in you."

"I'll try," I said. I was back on the couch, not under the quilt, but lying there, in my clothes. When she brought me the cup and saucer, I sat up, putting my feet on the floor, and let a trickle down my throat. I could manage the tiniest of sips.

"Good," Grandma said.

"Thanks," I said. "For taking me to the clinic. And everything. Looking after me."

Grandma sat down by the window, cradling her own cup of tea. "I never was much good at it before. Taking care of people. I just didn't seem to have it in me when I was younger; didn't have the patience for looking after anything, even my own children." She circled the rim of her teacup with her finger. "And I didn't understand how much my girls still needed me when I up and left, even though they were close to being grown. My husband not your grandpa — but the man I'm married to now, he taught me about caring. He had a stroke not too many years after I married him, and I finally realized what it meant to stick by someone who isn't always what you want them to be. I don't know why it took me so long. I guess I'm a slow learner."

She took a drink of her tea. "So I'm glad Pearl called me here to help. To be with you until she felt a little better. Especially since you're sick. A sick child needs looking after."

"I'm hardly a child, Grandma." Now that we were alone, I wanted her to tell me so much, about her and Pearl, and what had happened, and why no one had ever told me those things before. Why there were so many secrets.

She stared at me for a long time, then looked around the dusty living room. In the silence that stretched between us, the house seemed to be murmuring its own story — hot air whispering through the floor vent behind the television, the quiet but insistent droning of the fridge in the kitchen, the sighing of water in the pipes in the wall behind me.

Grandma's profile was outlined by the light from the window behind her head. I brought my heels up on to the edge of the couch, and tucked my knees up under my chin, still holding my tea.

"No, Mercy, I can see that you aren't a child. Neither was your mother, when I left home so long ago. When I think back, it seems she never was a child. Always so serious, quiet. Intense, I guess. Who knows why? And then there's Maureen. Seems like she never really grew up. Two kids, same parents, different as could be." She made a noise in the back of her throat, almost like a snap — the sound her purse made when she closed it. And from that sound I could tell she wasn't going to tell me any more about the past.

"And now here you are, caught in between them." She looked around again, her chest rising and falling, inhaling and then exhaling, in long, almost sorrowful, breaths.

"Some things just keep on repeating," she said. "Cycles. Things passed on. You see and hear about it all the time now, on those television talk shows."

I bent my face into the tea's steam, hoping Grandma would think the flush I felt start in my cheeks was from the rising heat. I was ashamed, and angry at her, for what I knew she was thinking. And I didn't want her to think that Pearl had made a mistake with me.

"Not only negative things are passed on," I said, lifting my face to meet hers. "There are a lot of good traits that can be inherited, too. Like the way you taught Moo about tea leaves. Like the way Pearl was so interested in words, and got me interested, too. How Moo helped me learn to love reading."

"Right you are, my girl," she said. "Right you are. And you've inherited a good strong trait from your mother. That backbone of yours."

I sat up straighter.

"You'll do fine, Mercy, with whatever you do. I can see that. And it's because you've inherited your mother's grit."

"It hasn't done much good for her." I gripped the china edge of the teacup between my teeth.

"'No." Grandma looked toward the window. "It appears she got a little sidetracked. But from what I know of her, she'll get back on. She just needs some help. I think she's going to have to learn to take it. Help. It's like love. When it's offered, you reach out the other half of the way and take it. Don't hold back out of some silly pride. It's hurtful for a person not to acknowledge love, or help, when it's genuinely offered."

At the sound of footsteps outside, she pulled aside the curtain. "Here comes Maureen. She must have really hurried to be back so soon. Surprising she could move so fast with her weight."

She got up and went into the kitchen. "You really flew, didn't you?" I heard her ask, after the door opened.

"Did I make good time? I went as fast as I could. It's hard walking on the sidewalks; they're so slushy. Is that tea for me?"

"I couldn't have done it any quicker myself," Grandma answered. "Good for you. And yes, here's your tea. It's still hot. Just the way you like it; at least the way you used to like it. No milk, two sugars. Am I right?"

"You're right, Ma," Moo said, and they both came back into the living room, and the three of us sat politely, holding our cups and saucers, sipping quietly, Moo and Grandma talking about the weather. *Like a tea party,* I thought, although I've never actually been to one. The only comparison I had was Alice's tea party — the one with the March Hare and the Hatter and the Dormouse.

CHAPTER TWENTY-FIVE

❦

By the next afternoon my throat felt almost better, and my fever was completely gone.

"I can't believe the antibiotics can work so fast," I said, sitting at the kitchen table and drinking something Grandma had made for me — a delicious thick combination of vanilla ice cream and mashed-up bananas and an egg and some vanilla and a dash of chocolate syrup, all whipped to a milky froth. I was starving; I felt like I could eat forever, and Grandma had sent Moo out again for all kinds of things that were soft and easy to swallow — yoghurt, ice cream, and iced lollipops for me to suck on.

"But you still shouldn't go back to school tomorrow," Grandma said, chopping carrots into tiny squares. "It's too soon. Even though you might feel alright, your body's been through a bad time. Make sure you're all better, or you'll end up back in bed again. Trust me."

"I think I'll go to work for a few hours this evening though. Just one or two. I've hardly worked at all for the last few weeks. I need to make some money. And I can't keep expecting my boss to let me take time off. I can't believe he hasn't fired me."

Grandma scooped up a handful of the chopped carrots and dropped them into the boiling soup.

"A few hours out might be a good way to start," she said, putting the lid on the soup pot. "And there's another reason you should stay home tomorrow."

I tipped the glass up to my lips, tapping on the bottom to urge the last few drops of the milk shake into my mouth.

"Your mother will be coming home. They're releasing her about eleven. So it would be nice if you were here to greet her."

I set the glass on the table and went to take a shower. I didn't want to think about it.

Later, at work, Mama Gio asked me about my mother. "How's you mama? She doing any more good now?"

Vince glanced at me. "Mama," he said, rattling something off at her in Italian and shaking his head no.

Mama Gio's beads clanked. "Is okay, Vince. We talk, Mercy and me."

"She's coming home tomorrow," I said, wiping down one of the glass doors.

"You want some help? I could bring the truck around." Vince said.

I thought about what Grandma had said. About taking what people offer. "Okay. That would be great," I said. "My aunt was going to take a cab to the hospital. Would you mind coming around to pick her up first? You've met her. Maureen."

Grandma and I were waiting in the kitchen.

When Vince and Moo and Pearl came in the back door, my mother looked small and sad between them. I even imagined that the air around her had a grey look. I wanted to hug her so badly. "Hi," I said, not moving.

"Come on in, my girl," Grandma said to Pearl. "I've made a nice minestrone soup. I remember how you liked minestrone once upon a time." She took a step toward Pearl, then stopped. The grey aura around Pearl seemed to have developed a texture, like the strange invisible armour that you see people inside of in movies about outer space. Everything looks normal until you try to touch the person, and then the barrier surrounds your hand like clear melted plastic. I was afraid to try. I was too afraid it would be real.

Pearl's mouth moved. "That's nice, Ma. Thanks. I just need to lie down for a bit."

"Of course, of course," Grandma said. "You just go on, now." She reached out one hand, again, as if she wanted to help Pearl, but then pulled it back. It seemed she was afraid of the armour, too.

"Here's her bag," Vince said, setting down a small case.

Pearl was already on her way down the hall.

"Thanks, Vince," Moo said. "For everything. Coming with me, picking up Pearl."

"It's nothing." He glanced at his wristwatch. "But I gotta run. Theresa can't stay too long at the store today."

Moo smiled. I realized that it was a weary, grown-up smile, not her usual silly one.

"You're sure you won't have a bowl of soup?" Grandma asked.

"No. But thank you, thank you anyway." He stuck his baseball cap back on his head. "So I'll see you at work tomorrow, Mercy?"

"Yeah," I said. "I'll be there."

"Ma," Moo said, "Vince says he has a rollaway cot at his place. He said he can bring it over in his truck, and put it in my room for you. Now that Pearl's home," she added.

Vince worked the zip of his jacket. "I can bring it over tonight."

"No," Grandma said. "Mercy's back in her room, so I'll just sleep on the sofa. You don't need to bother."

"No, Ma, you take my bed," Moo said. "I'll take the couch."

"Let's not argue about it now," Grandma said. "But don't worry about the cot. We won't need it."

"Okay, then," he said.

"Good-bye, Vincent," Moo said.

Vince lifted his head from his zip as if he'd just caught a whiff of his favourite pie baking. "It's actually Vincenzo." He said it the Italian way, making the *c* a *ch*.

"Well, good-bye then, Vin*ch*enzo," Moo said.

"Yeah. We'll be seeing you, Maureen," he answered.

We didn't talk much while we ate the soup. It was good, thick and hot. There was a lot of barley in it, and carrots and shredded cabbage and kidney beans.

Later I put some into a bowl, and took it down the

hall to Pearl's room. I knocked. "Pearl? I brought you some soup. Can I come in?"

There was a faint sound that I took for a yes. I got the door open and stepped inside. "The soup is great," I said, putting the bowl on the dresser. "You should eat it."

"I will soon," Pearl said. She was lying on top of her bed, on her back, looking at the ceiling. "I was just thinking how good my own bed feels."

"Grandma washed your bedding this morning," I said.

"I know. I can smell the fabric softener." She turned her face toward me, then her eyes moved to the table beside her bed. I followed her eyes, and saw the yellow mask propped up against the wall.

"It's such a pretty colour," she said. "So bright. Yellow is my favourite colour."

"Is it? I didn't know that."

Pearl kept looking at the mask. "I don't think I did, either, until yesterday. I kept looking at it, and realized what a beautiful colour yellow is."

I made a sound.

"Maureen told me Barry wouldn't be back," Pearl said.

I nodded.

"I'm glad," she said.

"Me, too."

"You were right all along," Pearl said. "He was creepy."

"But what about the money?"

"That's not your problem. The sweater looks the way I thought it would," she said, still not looking at me. "It's so good to see you in something besides black."

I put one hand on my caramel-coloured sleeve. I had worn the sweater for her. I was so glad that she even noticed; it meant she was seeing me, even if she was looking at the mask. I felt that burning at the backs of my eyes again. It's not my problem, she had said, about the money.

Then she looked in my direction. "The sweater looks beautiful." When her eyes met mine, a funny, light feeling started swimming somewhere at the top of my head. Even though I knew she was talking about the sweater, I felt like she meant me.

I hoped my fever wasn't back.

CHAPTER TWENTY-SIX

❦

When I came downstairs the next morning, Grandma already had her sheets and blankets folded and stacked on the end of the couch. She was holding a framed school picture of me when I was in grade four, the one that sat on the television. Grandma pulled a tissue out of the sleeve of her blouse and wiped off the glass. She had cleaned the whole house over the last few days, dusting and vacuuming and washing.

"You look as if you're feeling a lot better," she said. "You actually have some colour in your cheeks."

"I do feel almost normal. I'm going back to school today."

"But make sure you take all the antibiotics. Don't stop, just because you feel better. Remember, you have to take them right to the last pill."

"I will," I said.

She looked back at the picture in her hand. "I wish I'd known you when you were a little girl," she said, as if she were talking to the girl under the glass. She set the picture back, smiling as if I weren't there. "And just look at that hair." Slowly her head turned toward me. "Is it still that colour? That beautiful red-gold?"

I heard someone moving around in the kitchen.

The clink of dishes, and the slow drip of the coffee-maker. Then whistling. Moo, whistling one of the old songs she likes. It was James Taylor, "You've Got a Friend," I think.

"Yeah," I said, bending my head and pulling my hair apart, "you can tell by my roots." I had noticed the thin strip of colour when I was combing through it after I washed it yesterday. With all that had happened, I hadn't thought about getting my usual supply of black dye for the last while.

"I hope I get to see it sometime," she said, "the real colour. Mine was red, too, but darker." She stepped back toward the couch. I saw her flowered bag open on the floor. My heart gave one low thump of dread.

"You're not going, are you?" I asked, even though I knew that the open bag, clothes folded neatly inside, could only mean one thing.

"There's a bus leaving at two this afternoon."

I crossed my arms over my chest. "But I don't want you to go." I said it without thinking. I hadn't thought about her going, or staying. "It felt good, Grandma. You looking after me. After us all."

"I know, dear. I know. But if I stay, you'll keep on needing me. And then Pearl won't have anyone to need her."

I looked out into the hall, at Pearl's closed door. "But she never let me need her. She always made me do things for myself. She told me it was better that way, not to depend on anyone. It will only be worse now. Please stay, Grandma."

Grandma shook her head. Her mouth was a soft, straight line, like one of the threads of pink wool that ran through her mittens. "It's time for me to go."

"But it feels wrong." I clenched my back teeth together. "Why?" She sat on the couch and patted the space beside her.

I sat down.

"I've written my address and phone number, and left them beside the phone. I expect you to write. I get the feeling you would write a good letter. If there's something really urgent, you just pick up the phone and call, collect. And if that boss of yours gives you any time off this summer, well then, you just hop on a bus and come for a visit."

She put her arm around me, and I rested against her. I smelled two of my favourite smells: lavender and cinnamon. I suddenly remembered that Pearl used to smell of cinnamon.

"But you're the Queen of Cups," I said, my voice almost a whisper.

"What did you say?"

I sat up. "The Queen of Cups. Remember? Moo called you that the first night you arrived. She had read it in her tarot cards. She read hers, and Pearl's, and mine, and we all drew the Queen of Cups. It's a strong, wise woman. She sees visions in a cup. And then she takes chances, and makes them happen. She makes them come true."

"And you think I'm that woman?"

I nodded. "Everything's been better since you've been here. It all feels changed."

"Changes go on all the time," Grandma said. "Just like Maureen's tea leaves. Her cards. Every day there are changes of some kind." Grandma smoothed my hair behind my ears.

"It's not me," she told me. "I'm not the Queen of Cups. I've made too many mistakes through my life. Most of my choices have been poor ones. Come to think of it, my visions were pretty cloudy. No, it's not me who has the ability to see things and make them real. I failed in a lot of ways. Like with your mother."

"But you said it was Pearl. Pearl wouldn't give you a second chance."

"But it was also me that didn't try hard enough. Reach out far enough." She stretched her hand forward, into the air. "Remember what I said? That you have to reach at least halfway. At least halfway." She pulled her hand back and rested it on her thigh. "It's too bad it took so long for me to realize that it was up to me to reach out, too. To Pearl. Not just wait for her. But I know now. And I'm not going to let go again."

In the kitchen, Moo's whistling had turned into a quiet, whispery kind of singing, the kind you do without thinking, but that you do only when you're feeling alright.

"So you're saying there is no Queen of Cups?"

Grandma pressed her lips together, and took my chin in her fingers. "Of course there is."

I looked into her eyes. I could see myself in her pupils, my head big compared to my neck and shoulders. That's all I could see. Me.

"The Queen of Cups is right here," Grandma said.

CHAPTER TWENTY-SEVEN

❦

The next day, Andrea invited me for supper. I hadn't been to her house since the day Pearl had gone to the hospital. So much had happened in that time — my birthday, me getting sick, Grandma showing up, Pearl coming home again. And, of course, Barry's arrival, and his departure.

"I don't think so," I told her. We were standing outside the main doors at lunchtime. The air smelled clean and new.

"Please, Mercy. You haven't been over for so long. And you've never eaten at our place. My mom is making lasagne. Hers is really good." She held her bag of crisps out to me. "I need to tell you something. Something unbelievable." Her eyes were bigger and rounder than I'd ever seen.

"I have a ton of homework," I told her, taking a crisp, "because of the days I missed when I was sick."

"It's really, I mean really, something great, Mercy. And you told me you don't have to work. You could just stay for supper, then go home. Please? I feel like celebrating." She stopped, her smile fading. "Sorry. I wasn't thinking. Is it your mom? Do you have to go and see her? At the hospital?" She was so trusting. It almost made me sad, the way she was looking at me, so concerned, biting her lips.

"No, it's not that," I said. "Actually, my mom is home

"Oh." Andrea put another crisp to her lips, but didn't bite it. "Is she, you know, okay?"

"Not yet," I said. "But she's better than before. It takes awhile when," I hesitated, "when you've had a breakdown."

"Yeah. I guess it would." We both looked at the bag of crisps in her hand, stretched toward me. I reached in and took another one.

Andrea was offering more than potato crisps. She was still offering me her friendship, even though I hadn't given her much in return. "Actually, it would probably be alright with my mother if I do go to your house. I'll give her a call and let her know. So, yeah, I'll come."

"Great! I'll meet you here, after last class. Wait until I tell you what's happened!" And she gave this funny little kick in the air, and then was gone.

When I went to the front doors after school, Andrea wasn't there. Starr and Monique were, though. I stopped, my hand on the door handle, when I saw them standing there. They were talking to two guys. I didn't know one of them. The other one's name was Sasha. He was in my geography class, and we'd had to do a project about Portugal together. He was kind of shy, but had a quiet, quirky sense of humour.

I watched Starr and Monique talking, showing perfectly straight teeth when they laughed, and swinging around their bouncy, probably smells-like-a-spring-meadow hair. I could wait inside for

Andrea, where they wouldn't see me. Andrea had to come this way. I watched them for another minute, then took a deep breath and pushed the door open.

I walked past the little group and leaned against the railing at the wide front steps. I counted. One one thousand, two one thousand, three one thousand. It took Starr and Monique exactly six seconds to launch their attack.

"Hey, Morticia, boiled up anything up lately?" Monique called. "Any frogs?"

I looked at her. "Are you talking to me?"

"Do you see any other ghouls around?"

"My name is Mercy."

The boy I didn't know made a sound in his throat that could have been an embarrassed laugh. Or it might have been a frog of his own.

Starr put her hand on his arm. "Tyler, you should know this." She pointed at me. "Her aunt is a gypsy; she can put spells on you. Love potions, cures for bad breath, you name it."

The boys shuffled their feet. "Leave her alone," Sasha said.

"It's okay," I said. "They'll be finished in a few seconds. In case you haven't noticed, they don't have very long attention spans."

Starr's mouth dropped open. "Sasha! Don't let her talk to me like that."

"Grow up, okay, Starr?" he said. Then he looked right at me. I remembered how, when we'd been working on the project together, we'd somehow started talking about ice cream. We discovered that we had the exact same favourite — tiger tiger in a sugar cone that had the edges dipped in chocolate; no nuts.

Andrea came through the doors. "Sorry I'm late, Mercy. Ready?"

"Sure," I answered. I smiled at Sasha; he smiled back. I didn't look at Starr, but I knew she was furious.

"Come on," Andrea said. "It's faster if we cut through the parking lot."

On the way through the parking lot behind the school we jumped over the puddles that lay in all the depressions in the gravel. I noticed a rusting red pick-up truck because the driver's door was open, and someone was sitting inside, head on her arms, resting on the steering wheel. Just as we walked past the open door, she raised her head. It was Mrs Hardy-Spade.

"Oh, hi, Mercy," she said.

We stopped. "Hi," I answered.

"I'm waiting for the Motor League to get here. I can never rely on this old beater."

I saw greasy taco wrappers on the seat. A dirty hockey sweater was crumpled on the floor.

"I share it with my two sons," Mrs Hardy-Spade said. "And it always happens like this. It never breaks down except on the days I have it. Just my luck." She sighed. "So, are things still fabulous for you?" She took off her glasses and rubbed her eyes, then put the glasses back on.

"Not entirely," I said.

"Remember my room number?"

"117."

She nodded, and I nodded back, and Andrea and

I went on our way. At her house, we got some crackers and grapes from the kitchen.

"Supper at five thirty," Andrea's mother said, tearing up lettuce at the sink. "I'm glad you're staying, Mercy."

Andrea pulled my arm. "Let's go to my room." Once we were out of the kitchen, she whispered, "I'm bursting to tell you this. Come on. And it's not a secret or anything. It's okay if I tell. As of last weekend, it's official."

When we were both sitting on Andrea's bed, she took one grape and popped it in her mouth. "Are you ready for this?"

I nodded, fingering the square edges of the cracker in my hand.

"It's my dad. He's coming back!" She bit the grape, smiling and watching me.

"Coming back to live?"

"Well, not in this house, not yet, but he's leaving Vancouver and coming to rent an apartment downtown here. And my mom said they're just going to take it slow; see how it goes. See how it goes, Mercy! That's almost like saying they're getting back together."

She bounced up and down on the bed, smiling, then put another grape in her mouth. "They've been talking on the phone for hours every night all month. I can't imagine the phone bill. I knew something was up, but my mom wouldn't say anything. And then, when I got home from your birthday on Friday, he was here. He just stayed for the weekend, and flew back to pack up his stuff." She stopped for a gasp of air.

A warmth was spreading up from my chest on to my neck and into my cheeks. I didn't know why. After all, it was Andrea's good news, not mine. "That's great, Andrea. That is more than great. It's stupendous."

"I know, I know. I really, really want my dad to move back in. I mean, I think that's what every kid always dreams about, right? They make movies about it all the time — that when your parents separate, they still really love each other and will get back together again. They never do in the movies, at least not in modern ones, because then it seems too unreal, and they want kids to know that real life isn't perfect. But sometimes it is!" She was bouncing faster and faster, in time to her words. All of a sudden she stopped.

"Oh, Mercy. I'm sorry. My mother says I can be insensitive. I just was, wasn't I? I mean," she stopped. "I wasn't thinking about you. I'm sorry," she said again.

I leaned toward her and gave her a hug, my arms around her shoulders. When I touched her, she looked as surprised as I felt. "Hey, Andrea, you should be happy. I'm happy for you." I realized I was. It felt good to feel something for someone else for a change.

CHAPTER TWENTY-EIGHT

❦

A Sunday afternoon in April; we're into the third week, and it's spring, no going back now. After its lion start, March decided to humour us and go out like a lamb.

As I walked home from picking up some groceries, my feet felt light on the cement sidewalk, even though I was wearing the same boots I'd worn all winter. It reminded me of when I was a little girl, and could finally take off my winter boots and wear runners out to play; I remembered the sensation of running and skipping, no longer weighed down by the clunky weight on my feet.

I walked along the slant of the uneven paving blocks that led to the back of the house, stopping for a minute to look at the old tree still lying across our yard. It looked pitiful: one thick, broken branch sticking straight up, like it was going under for the third time and silently calling for help.

The door was open; I could hear voices.

"You're just in time for some cake, Mercy," Moo said, as I came in. "Vincenzo and his mother brought it over."

"Hi, Vince," I said, not entirely surprised to see him there. Moo had stopped in at Santa Marie one day a few weeks ago, and talked to Vince for a while, eating two chunks of brownie during her stay. Then, a few days after that, Vince had driven me home because it was pouring rain. I had told him about a leak in the kitchen ceiling, and mentioned how there would probably be a flood in there now, and he'd come in with me and had a look at it. The next day he showed up, and had gone up on the roof and replaced a few shingles. Another time he'd phoned to check on my work schedule, but Moo had answered, and they ended up talking for at least ten minutes before she'd handed me the phone.

Now, on the kitchen table was a high, round cake, swirled with white icing and decorated with miniature, purple violets. The brown teapot and Moo's white tea-reading cups and saucers were there, too, along with small plates and forks covered with crumbs and smears of icing. It all sat on a tablecloth, an old green and white checked one that I remembered from some other kitchen table, long ago. There was a delicious smell in the air. Cinnamon.

When I looked at Mama Gio, I realized she was asleep, her head resting on her hand. I put the groceries away while Moo bustled around the kitchen, taking another plate from the cupboard. "Just look at that cake! Isn't it something? Vince baked it."

"*Buon giorno,* Mercy," Mama Gio said, suddenly lifting her head, her eyes focusing on me.

"*Buon giorno,*" I answered.

"And look at what your mother did today," Moo said to me, pointing at a square glass pan on the counter. "Apple-cinnamon coffee cake. She made it this morning. We were waiting for you to get home to cut into it, but then Vince stopped by with this one. Two cakes in one day! It's either feast or famine in this house." She beamed at me.

The apple-cinnamon coffee cake was like the tablecloth; I remembered it from some time and place long ago.

"Your auntie's been telling me about Donnelly's Desserts," Vince said. "And I've been telling her about my empty place, a couple of doors down from Santa Marie."

"The one with the stained glass window? You own that?"

"Yeah. And the carpet place, too. I bought all three buildings years ago, before the street got so popular, when all those places were cheap. The street could sure use a place to get something to eat."

I looked at Moo as she handed me my cake. Her eyes were shining, and clear.

There was a creak from the hall, and I looked to see Pearl's door opening slowly. As I watched, she came out. She was still pale, but her hair was brushed, and she had on a denim shirt; the collar was open, and I could see the glint of dark beads at her throat. She gave me a little wave, then headed toward the bathroom.

I looked down at the plate in my hand. "You mean you do all the baking?" I asked Vince. "Not your mother?"

Mama Gio made her laughing sound. "I make Italian food. Italians no eat so much sweet. Maybe fruit for dessert. But my Vince, he a Canadian boy now. He like sweet. So he make it."

I saw my mother heading back to her room. I put my cake down and went into the hall. When I passed the living room, I saw that there was a glass vase filled with yellow tulips on a doily in the middle of the coffee table. One of the tulips arched gently downward, and the sun seemed to be caught and reflecting in that cup-shaped bloom. The television was on, but tuned to the weather channel, with the volume turned low. I could just make out the sound of violins.

Pearl had left her door open. She was looking out the window, and turned when she heard me come in.

"Can you help me get this up?" she asked. "I don't think it's been opened since we moved in. I hope it's not painted shut. The room feels so stuffy."

It took a few bangs and tugs, but eventually we got the window open. It creaked and complained as we pushed together, and then it stopped, halfway. "That's alright," Pearl said. "Partway is alright for now."

A fresh, warm, breeze swept into the room. I saw Pearl lift her chin, and her nostrils widened.

"See that spot?" I asked, pointing at the strip of dry grass along the back of the yard. "That's where I'm putting in a flower bed. Perennials and annuals. Vince said I can take whatever I want from the stuff he brings in from the greenhouse to sell. As soon as the tree is gone and the ground is softer, we're going to dig it up. And then I can start planting the Perennials in May. There won't be that many flowers this year, though. Perennials take a few years to get settled, Vince says. But once they get their roots down, they'll bloom for years."

"Uh-huh," Pearl said.

"So by next summer it will be pretty full. Vince said it could look like a wild English garden."

Pearl just kept looking out the window. "That's a long time away," she finally said. "Next summer. Maybe we shouldn't count on it."

"It's not that long." I studied the shattered wood of the old fence. "It's the immediate future."

Pearl ran her finger along one edge of the windowsill. "Look at this dust. I miss Ma for that; she was always good at keeping everything clean." There were a few seconds of silence. "I guess I could start with this room," she added.

I watched her, narrowing my eyes so that I could block out everything else and concentrate on her face through the tunnel. It didn't work. I blinked, and tried again until my forehead hurt, tried to get only her face in focus and close out the rest of the room. But I kept seeing everything, all of her, her denim shirt and necklace and, behind her, the recipe book lying open on the smooth bedspread, the page showing fan-shaped cookies with the name "Madeleines" at the top. I saw the: plate with only a thin wedge of Vince's cake left on it, and Pearl's ticking wind-up clock, and the lamp, and the yellow mask propped against it.

I put my finger into the dust on the sill in front of me. "I can help you," I said. And with my finger, I made an *M,* for Mercy, in the layer of soft dust. Then I made another, and, between them, a small circle. *M O M,* I spelled.

I took my cake out to the backyard and sat on the trunk of the fallen tree. I'd left the back door open, and I could hear Vince and Moo washing dishes, laughing and trying to sing something that sounded vaguely like opera in a mixture of Italian and English. Every once in a while, Mama Gio's high, trembling voice broke in. It seemed I could still smell cinnamon wafting out to where I was sitting, although Pearl had baked her cake hours earlier. I took a bite of Vince's cake. It was moist, and lemony; so good that for some reason it made my throat ache when I swallowed it. But it was nothing like the ache from my strep throat. This was a different, sweet kind of ache.

There was a movement from my mother's window, and then another. She was spraying the inside of the window, and wiping it with a cloth. The cloth went back and forth, from top to bottom, slowly but thoroughly. When she was finished, she looked through the shining glass, then waved with the cloth. I waved back.

I tilted my head up to look at my own window, right above hers. The sun was warm on my face. I saw nooks and crannies near the roof that I had never seen before, and, in a small protected hollow under the eaves, I saw a bird. It was the pigeon, back again, even after all the times I shooed her away last month. This time she had a little stick in her beak. She was busy making a nest. There were twigs and bits of newspaper piled up. The pigeon was building her nest against the wall, using my home to help make her own.

I took another bite of my cake, and then crumbled what was left on to the rough bark of the fallen tree.

Later, when I was in my mother's room, I turned off the vacuum. "Look," I said, pointing through the open window at the tree, at the pigeon sitting there, greedily pecking at the cake crumbs. "There. On the tree. Maybe more will come."

"It looks a lot like Frank," my mother said, putting down the clean sheets and coming to stand beside me.

"I know," I answered, and I felt the warmth of her arm, resting against mine.